ISBN-13 (mobi): 978-1-7781998-4-4
ISBN-13 (epub): 978-1-7781998-5-1
ISBN-13 (paperback): 978-1-0691233-0-5

Cover design by: Claris Lam
Library of Congress Control Number: 2018675309
Printed in the United States of America

BLOODY FANTASIA

Claris Lam

CHAPTERS

CHAPTER 1

Aubri Harlow knew that her twin sister, Aria, wasn't much like her at all.

Aria Hawthorn was quiet and preferred hiding in her room to socializing with others. She savoured text messages, tweets, and emails over in-person interaction and phone calls. She also preferred writing poetry and short stories than give speeches or start conversations. Aubri, meanwhile, would have a tough time writing any short stories or poems, and enjoyed any conversation she could have with someone face-to-face.

Aria flinched at most mentions of murder. She would rather pretend she didn't hear about them if she didn't have to. Aubri – despite *everything* she went through at this point – kept an interest in reading murder mysteries and keeping up with related shows and podcasts. She didn't think she would continue having such an interest, given the danger involved with investigating them – but she did anyway, and that was just something she accepted by this point.

Aria and Aubri also had two different fathers. Neither of them knew only until six months ago due to their mother, Geneva Harlow, hiding it from them until several months ago. Aubri hadn't spoken to her mother since then, but she knew that Aria kept in contact with her. It still felt wrong, in Aubri's opinion, that her mother kept her affair with the late Leighton Faulkner a secret from her and her twin sister for such a long time.

Aria, meanwhile, willingly stayed connected to the family members she had. Aubri supposed it made sense on Aria's end. After all, Aria grew up never really knowing Geneva before learning she and Aubri had different fathers. Aria previously lived with Aubri's biological father all their lives since both parents had custody of one twin child after divorcing. Losing Leighton, her actual biological father, probably gave Aria good reason to stay in contact with whatever family she still had left. It was what prompted Aria to live with Aubri now, and Aubri was grateful for that despite the circumstances that led to it.

However, Aubri knew one family member well, and that was one Bastian Faulkner - the same man who fake-dated Aubri back when both attended university together. He was also, as revealed months ago, technically Aria Hawthorn's biological uncle due to Leighton's affair with Geneva (which made him

Aubri's half-uncle). At least Bastian's life was at ease now, after settling things with his father post-Leighton's demise. Aubri wasn't oblivious to the fortune Bastian inherited from Leighton, and he likely had millions of dollars on him after selling the mansion he also inherited if not billions. Despite his riches, Bastian made it clear that he wasn't about to go wild with all the money he now had, preferring to keep a more low-key life.

But what about Aubri herself? She now had a half-uncle and a twin sister, as well as said half-uncle's boyfriend, Nick, as a friend. Sure, it might be awkward living with all three of them at the same time, even if they now lived in apartments right across from each other. However, at least it was *something* good going on in her life.

The only thing she didn't like about living with Aria was her constant violin playing. When Aubri asked Aria about it, Aria explained that she was practicing for an audition for a top-notch music school. Aubri didn't mind Aria's playing, but she feared angering the neighbours. They went to the lengths of taping blankets to the walls or throwing any spare comforters and pillows into Aria's room so she could practice and muffle the sound enough to not disturb anyone else.

Aria was skilled at the violin. Aubri was no music expert, but Aria's music sounded quite nice. Aubri only grew up learning some piano, and briefly some violin in high school, but that was it. Aria had better musical talent between the two of them for sure.

It was no surprise to Aubri, then, that Aria received an offer of acceptance into the music school called the Da Capo Music Institution. And tomorrow, she would be moving into the dorm room of the school. The plan was to get to the school via train. Bastian and Nick (who took the week off work) promised to help them move Aria's things into the dorm.

Aubri made sure to spend tonight helping Aria finish packing. After most of it was done, Aubri decided to take Aria out for some late-night dessert, buying chocolate parfaits for both. It was a sweet reward for all the packing they did for the journey ahead. Taking the train to the music school would only take a few hours. But Aubri knew that she had to help Aria carry a lot to her dorm room.

"I still can't believe I made it in." Aria mused as the two ate their parfaits. She took a scoop of her own, devouring it, before continuing to speak. "The Da Capo Music Institution is pretty competitive, so I'm really surprised about it still."

"You're really good with your violin playing, though." Aubri managed, offering her a soft smile. "Why did you decide to enter, anyway? It was for..." She tried to remember, "Music production and composition, right?"

A soft smile spread across Aria's face. "Yeah, that's it! But to get in, you have to audition with an instrument or by singing. It's required for every student, no matter what you want to study. And this school is *prestigious*."

"Prestigious, huh?" Aubri thought of the boarding schools that she read of in some novels. "Do you have to wear uniforms?" After all, it wasn't uncommon to wear uniforms in private schools, or boarding schools.

"Surprisingly, no. Nothing like that. I mean, they have their school spirit wear, and everyone's expected to dress formally for most of the recitals and concerts. But there isn't any mandatory dress for normal classes." Aria shook her head with a light smile appearing on her face. "Think of it like a university, but it's exclusively for all areas of music. They even have a Pipe Organ program!"

"Really?" Aubri raised a brow. "Aren't pipe organs, like, old?"

"Yeah, they are. It's a miracle they exist today sometimes." She paused, sighing. "Besides, I'm sure the school is hurting for students right now. I think that helped me get in."

"Hurting? How?" Aubri ate a spoonful of her own parfait,

raising a brow. "Is it a lack of funding?" She wouldn't be surprised at any school lacking funding – especially one so entrenched in the arts.

"Well..." Aria paused, before lowering her voice. "Last year, there was a series of *murders* at that school. A lot of students were killed – and the past president was even murdered, too. Apparently, she was pushed off the roof to her death."

Aubri swallowed, the visions of her ex-girlfriend Renee Dimitri falling to her death and Leighton Faulkner's corpse bleeding out invading her mind's eye. She didn't want to see any more deaths if she didn't have to. The corpses from the last two cases still haunted her mind. She must have grimaced, because Aria's eyes flashed briefly, widening.

"I'm sorry." Aria managed, sighing. Aubri noticed Aria frowning as she continued speaking. "I shouldn't have explained so much in depth."

"Are you going to be okay over there?" Aubri asked, frowning. "Why go to a school where there are tons of murders, though? Why not, I don't know," She gestured in the air with her hand, "A normal school with no murders reported on campus?"

"There *were* murders. It's been about a *year* since that

happened." Aria corrected. "I'm sure they won't have it again, and they just got a new acting president. I doubt the entire school would shut down midway through my studies either. I'll be fine."

Aubri wasn't sure what to think of it. Attend a music school, where murders just recently happened? The murder-mystery fan inside of her wanted to check out this school even more, now, but the rest of her cautioned against knowing too much – because it led to too much danger. The various histories she'd uncovered, in the last two cases, was already a lot to cope with. Could she handle knowing more?

Then again, Aubri supposed that ignorance never helped anyone. She might not have a choice. Besides, she had to support her sister. If it meant learning a little bit about the music school's bloody history, she could bear with it. Besides, if that history stayed in the past and didn't repeat, things would be fine. Right?

CHAPTER 2

The next day, Aubri and Aria packed up Aria's things, and went on the train with Bastian and Nick. The train ride was only a few hours from their town to the music school. In addition to moving Aria's things in, this day was also the Welcome/ Orientation Day for all the new students. Aubri learned of this from Aria; there would be tours of the school, and even a scheduled welcoming ceremony presenting the new acting president, including a recital from the school's current students.

"You've heard about that school's history with murder, right?" Bastian quipped, lowering his voice so the other people on the train wouldn't hear. He still dyed his silvering hair on occasion, but he must've forgotten this time – Aubri saw a few grey strands peeking out close to the roots.

Aria nodded. "I already know." She managed. "But it's in the past, right? It's just those murders from the previous year. I'm sure they'll be more careful with security."

"I'm sure, but…" Bastian leaned back in his seat, "I did

a little digging, and apparently there were murders from about twenty years ago, too. There wasn't a lot of info about those ones, but still…"

Nick suddenly went still, his gaze snapping towards Bastian. Aubri noticed that Nick seemed slightly paler in the moment, golden-brown eyes widening. His shoulders tensed as he asked, "Twenty?"

"Yeah." Bastian looked towards him, frowning lightly. "Are you okay? You seem a little pale."

"No, I'm fine. I guess…" A brief, sheepish chuckle left Nick before he shook his head. He seemed calmer now, shoulders relaxing. "I-I guess I'm just nervous from all those previous murders, you know. It's not fun."

"Fair point." Bastian wrapped a reassuring arm around Nick's shoulders, squeezing him lightly in his grasp. "I'm sure it won't be like last time."

"Thanks." Nick offered Bastian a soft smile, before leaning his head against his shoulder. Aubri envied the two and how happy they were together – just a little. Despite the age gap between Nick and Bastian, the two of them made their relationship work well. Now that they lived in the same apartment, both working steady jobs (Nick, despite the horrible experience of his first shift being a bartender on a train where an actual murder happened, stayed with that job while Bastian continued working from home) and getting closer day by day. Aubri was happy for them.

"How soon will we get there?" Aubri asked Aria, who offered her a smile.

"I think we have at least another one and a half hours." She managed, brushing a few strands of hair out of her face. "In the meantime, we just have to wait. Right?"

The train soon blared an announcement that they were still on-schedule to reach their destination. Aubri watched Aria's shoulders tremble a bit, and she took a deep breath, shaking her head.

"I just...." Aria started, stopped then started again, meeting Aubri's gaze, "I'm a little worried. What if the other students there think I'm weird? I've heard that the school's students are more competitive than the programs themselves, but..."

"I'm sure you'll fit in fine!" Aubri did her best to reassure her, offering her a smile. The last thing she needed was her own sister worrying so much about fitting in with the other students. "I mean, you're great at what you do."

Aria's brows furrowed as she glanced up at her. "But it's not like I won any competitions or anything important. Some of those students were child prodigies."

"That was when they were *children*. It could be different now." Aubri stated, and she watched Aria chuckle a little.

"Maybe it is." Silence fell between them afterward, but Aubri took the opportunity to just enjoy the train ride on the way to the school. It might be hectic trying to move everything in, so it was best to enjoy the peace now while she could.

CHAPTER 3

Nick knew about this music school before, even before Aria ever auditioned for it. He went there for a field trip, back when he was just a kid in elementary school. He didn't want to think about how that went. Back then, there wasn't a train station only five minutes away from the music school. Things had changed, but the past could not.

The campus looked exactly as he expected it to look: its own university campus, with large, towering buildings. Off in the distance, to the right of the main building and closer to a woodsy area, he noticed a large church. He couldn't see much of its details from how far away he was from the church right now, but it was lovely with the stained glass. He never got to go there on his field trip, all those years ago. Maybe this time would be different.

Relax, Nick. He told himself, taking a deep breath. *It'll be fine. It's not like twenty years ago. Or last year.*

He knew too well about the cases from twenty years ago.

But today was Aria's move-in day, and he didn't want to spoil the fun by mentioning his involvement in it to her. It was true that he was jumpy about all the murder cases, as he mentioned back on the train with the others. He didn't exactly *like* that he got stuck in two murder cases because he was there when they happened, after all. He willed himself to ignore it, shaking his head slightly, as he kept up pace with Bastian and the others.

"Are you sure you're okay, Nick?" Nick looked up towards Bastian, and then up ahead, realizing that Bastian had let Aubri and Aria go ahead of them so they could talk. They were in the main courtyard area now, just a large set of steps away from entering the main building. "You've been a bit antsy since our train ride on the way here."

Nick hesitated – he didn't want to mention it to Bastian, but...he also knew his lover could be persistent, when it came to matters concerning him or anyone he cared for. How else would Bastian have the courage to save him from Renee, during the time they met at the resort, and even look out so closely for Aubri and Aria? At least it wasn't like he had to tell Aria and Aubri to their faces about it. And Bastian did literally save Nick's life, after all, when they first met.

"I'm not okay." Nick finally admitted, taking a deep breath as he looked up at Bastian. He swallowed, thinking of the cases, before speaking. "When Aria mentioned the murders from last year…I need to come clean to you about this, but don't tell Aria and Aubri, okay? I want to do it myself when there's a better time. The murders Aria mentioned aren't the first ones that happened on this campus – I was there when the murders from twenty years ago happened."

"What?" Bastian raised a brow. "You were there?"

"Yeah. Back then, there was a string of murders that happened on campus. No one caught the killer at the time." Nick kept his voice low just in case there was anyone passing them by. "I was only a kid, but I was visiting the Da Capo Institution on a field trip with my classmates. I saw one of *those* murders, that day, with one of my other classmates after we got separated from the group. The only reason we got away with seeing them was because we hid before the murderer saw us."

"My goodness, Nick." Bastian shook his head, swallowing. "I'm sorry to hear that happened…"

"Yeah. I mean," He pushed bangs out of his face, "I know it happened years ago, and there aren't any murders happening *now.* But it's just…hard not to think about it occasionally."

"That explains it." Nick looked up in time for Bastian to kiss him on the forehead, and he felt himself relax a little. It was nice, knowing that his lover was here for him. "If you need to back out at any time during today if being here affects you badly, let me know."

"Thanks, Bastian." Nick tilted his own head up to give him a cheek kiss. "I appreciate it."

"Nick?" Nick pulled his head away from Bastian, turning on his heel to see a man approach him. Nick thought he recognized the other's voice. But it was seeing the other's deep brown eyes, light olive skin, and the familiar, light scar on the left side of his face that helped with truly recognizing him.

Nick hadn't seen him in years – not since elementary school. But if there was anyone else who would understand the unease of all those years ago, it was him.

"Akeno?" Nick whispered.

"Nick!" The man rushed over to Nick. A relieved, soft smile came to his face as he got close enough, stopping in his tracks – he pushed strands of whitish-blond hair out of his face. "It's been a while, hasn't it?"

"Wait, what?" Bastian looked between Nick, then Akeno, brows furrowing. "Sorry, have we met?"

"Oh, I don't think I've met *you* before. Sorry." Akeno turned to face Bastian, shaking his head, offering him a hand to shake. "I'm Akeno Botan. I'm teaching here as a TA – Nick and I know each other from elementary school, but we stayed connected on-and-off since."

"It's nice to meet you." Bastian offered Akeno a soft smile, shook his hand. "I'm Bastian."

"Nice to meet you, too." Akeno offered him an acknowledging nod. He let go of his hand, asking, "Are you a friend of his?"

"Bastian's my boyfriend." Nick blurted out, and he noticed Akeno's gaze snap towards him. "And an uncle to two friends of mine." He glanced toward Bastian with a sheepish grin. "Hope you don't mind me mentioning all that."

"It's fine." Bastian looked ready to laugh but suppressed his chuckles behind a smile. "It's going to be interesting introducing ourselves to everyone else we meet, explaining the relationships and all."

Akeno's eyes widened. Nick knew that he shouldn't be surprised by how shocking all of that sounded to him. If anything, seeing the other's reaction amused him. *"What?* Is all that true?"

Bastian offered Akeno a sheepish smile. "It's a long story. We can explain in depth later if you want."

Nick looked towards Akeno, who simply nodded awkwardly, before he spoke up. "Why are you here? I thought you graduated last year from the Piano program." He vaguely recalled seeing Akeno's graduation photos on social media from the other year.

"I did. However, the school hired me as a TA swiftly after graduation, for the new year." Akeno explained, shrugging lightly. "I admit I don't have all the qualifications, but the Institution is short-staffed. And despite what happened last year, I am grateful for getting a job here."

"Last year?" Nick asked. "Is that about the series of murders that went on during then…?"

"Yes." Akeno nodded once, a grim expression taking over his face. "After the institution dealt with the murderer, they had a challenging time finding new employees and students for this year. Most of the staff quit, and many students withdrew enrollment in their programs after that. I wasn't sure what to think of the job offer, but… here I am."

Nick paused, swallowing. "How are you holding up, er, since then?"

"I'm okay." Akeno reassured him. "As okay as I can be, at least." A sigh left him as he shook his head. "I'm glad I'm alive, but I wish my graduation ceremony hadn't included a memorial for the dead students. They could've been alive right now, if not for what happened back then."

"I'm sorry about your classmates." Nick swallowed lightly. "As for me, I'm just here for orientation day. A friend of mine, Aria, is a new student, so me, Bastian, and her sister are helping her move into the dorms."

"Aria? Do you mean by Aria Hawthorn, by any chance?" Akeno raised a brow. "I thought I overheard the other staff talking about her a while ago. Daughter of the late Leighton Faulkner, right? His murder was in the news for a short time."

Bastian visibly grimaced. "Yeah. And I'm Leighton's younger brother, by the way." Nick knew that Bastian and his brother had a messy history – one that would never quite feel resolved since Leighton was already dead. "It was...awkward."

"I see. You have my condolences for your brother." Akeno offered Bastian a soft, apologetic glance, before changing the subject. "What program is Aria in?"

"Strings." Nick answered quickly. "She plays the violin."

"I overheard the instructors that saw her audition." Akeno noted. His eyes glimmered with something Nick couldn't quite interpret – impressed, perhaps? Or intrigue? Perhaps both?

"They said she had very good technique."

Bastian smiled. "Really? I'll let her know that."

Someone bumped into his shoulder so forcefully that Nick almost tripped. He glanced towards the woman, not quite seeing her face but noticing her long, blonde hair tied back in a crisp ponytail, bangs obscuring her eyes from his.

"Sorry." The woman quipped quickly, before rushing off, her pace quickening as she made her way away from Nick and the others. She must be one of the staff, Nick guessed, just from seeing her crisp white blouse, black blazer and pencil skirt, and matching heels.

"What?" Bastian's gaze snapped towards the woman, eyes widening, before he looked towards Nick. He looked like he knew who it was. "Is she who I think she is?"

"Who do you think she is?" Nick frowned. "I didn't get a good look at her face."

"*I* did." Bastian looked towards Akeno, swallowing. "Sorry, but I need to talk to someone quickly. I'll catch up with both of you later if that's okay?"

Nick nodded. He didn't know who Bastian recognized that person from earlier to be, but he guessed it was someone important. He didn't want to stop him from catching up with whoever it was, and besides, Nick himself knew he had a lot to catch up on with Akeno. "Go. I'll see you later."

"It was nice meeting you." Akeno managed.

"Thanks." Bastian rushed off, half-running after the woman.

Akeno looked towards Bastian running off, and then towards Nick, a slight frown appearing on his face. "I wonder who he saw just now."

Nick shrugged. He didn't know, either. "Probably an old friend. I'm sure he'll catch up with us soon afterwards. Now..." He took a deep breath, looking Akeno in the eye. "I overheard there were murders at this school last year. How did that...go?"

He saw Akeno swallow, shoulders stiffening, and he shook his head. There was something haunted in his eyes, hollow at the very mention of the murders.

"I don't think that's something we should talk about. Not now. It's..." Akeno shook his head, and Nick found himself releasing a breath he didn't realize he was holding, as the other looked him in the eyes. "It's complicated. And this school would rather forget that it ever happened."

CHAPTER 4

Bastian raced into the school's main entrance, pushing past a few people, and apologizing as he did so. He knew it was perhaps a bit rude to leave Nick and Akeno behind, but he *knew* who that woman from earlier was. He knew when he last saw her. After trailing her down a few hallways, and into some emptier ones, he knew that it was now or never.

"Excuse me?" He called, and the woman stopped in her tracks, turning to look at him. "Lulu? Is that you?"

The woman's head turned to see him, her eyes widening, before a scowl appeared on her face.

"Shh!" She put a finger to her lips. Her familiar, annoyed glare appeared on her face, even behind the new pair of glasses she wore. Her blonde hair was in a neat, low ponytail. Instead of the fancy gear she wore, she now wore a plain pencil skirt, blouse, and vest to go with it. "No one knows that name around here, so don't say it in public! I go by my *real* name now, got it?"

Was she so annoying last time he saw her? He couldn't

remember, but he raised a brow at the mention of her real name. "And that is?"

"Louise Anders." A sigh left her, and she rolled her eyes, shaking her head. "It's *so* old-fashioned, I know. Don't laugh."

"And Bastian Faulkner isn't an old-fashioned name?" A soft laugh left Bastian, and he noticed her faintly smile. If it wasn't for the awkwardness of knowing that she used to be his dead brother's former friend-with-benefits, Bastian had a feeling that she and him would get along better. "Honestly, I'm surprised that you're here. How?"

She shrugged, taking a few steps towards him. "I got an offer to leave my old job, out of the blue. They needed new teachers and assistants, and an anonymous contact apparently recommended me for this position." A flicker of a smile appeared on her face again, just briefly, "I assumed it was *you* that did it, given that I was fuck buddies with your late brother and all, but..." She gestured towards him lightly with a wave of her hand, "I'm guessing you probably didn't recommend me if you didn't know how I got here, did you?"

"It was definitely not me." Bastian confirmed, frowning. *Someone anonymously recommended her?* "I haven't talked to you, or anyone related to you since what happened on the train six months ago! If I recommended you for anything, I would've let you know beforehand. And." He scratched the back of his head briefly, "I'm pretty sure I don't even have your phone number. So, it wasn't like I knew how to contact you as is."

"Fair." A sigh left Louise. "Well, whoever recommended me has my thanks. The pay's a lot better than I expected." She shrugged, before adding, "It's a lot different than my old job, but I have better health benefits and a higher salary, so I'm not complaining."

"I see." He supposed he was happy for her – who wouldn't want health benefits and good pay? Then again, he doubted that she was oblivious to this school's history. "You're aware of the previous murders at this school, I presume? Both from twenty years ago and last year?"

"Oh, totally. Both those pieces of info were all over the news when the murders happened last year – mainly the more recent ones, of course." She shuddered, shaking her head. "As long as *I'm* not dead by the time I'm done my job, I'm fine. Not so sure about those students, though. Why are you here? Enrolling, or?"

"Not me. I have little experience with music, and there's no way I'd make it in." He assured her. "Aria is, though. Me, Aubri, and Nick are here to help her move in."

"Aria Hawthorn? I thought I heard that she had some musical talent." Louise nodded lightly.

"Yeah." Bastian looked back towards the main hall, and then towards her. "Well, I guess we might run into each other on and off, but…good luck with your job here."

"Thanks." She offered him a soft smile. "I just wish you good luck not getting into more murder-case scenarios. You and your friends seem to keep encountering those for some reason."

He snorted lightly. "We'll see about that." He muttered, shaking his head.

A laugh left her, and he was glad about that. Being on friendly terms with her, despite the history between her and his late brother, was…kind of nice. "You can call me Lulu in private, but I prefer Louise otherwise. Got it?"

"Louise it is, then." Bastian concluded. "I'll see you later?"

"See you later." With that, she turned on her heel, leaving his sight. Bastian watched her go, smiling lightly, before deciding to find Aubri, Aria, and Nick.

CHAPTER 5

Aria knew she should be sticking around the main hall, but she also wanted to settle in. She did grab some school swag bags, filled with decorative buttons, pamphlets, and a map of the entire campus, but she also needed to put her things down in her room. She realized soon enough that Bastian and Nick must've gotten separated from them, and she and Aubri made their way to Aria's dorm room to put down everything before looking for them. As the two sisters made it to the dorm room, Aria noticed students already getting into their rooms with help from families. Both sisters carefully maneuvered their way past the surrounding people to reach her room.

"Do you have a roommate?" Aubri asked while Aria unlocked the door to her room.

"Not this year." Aria admitted. "I think it's due to a lack of enrollment." She didn't mind personally having her own room. It meant that she didn't have to share with someone else. A smile spread across her face as she let that thought sink in. Maybe she could invite Aubri over to her room to sleep over, if Aubri ever wanted to visit! "The room across me has two people, though."

As the sisters put down Aria's things, there was a soft knock on the door. Aria moved towards the door, opening it to see a woman standing there.

"Hi." The woman had to be about Aria's age, or maybe younger, given her youthful face. She brushed a few strands of thin, black hair out of her lighter brown eyes, swallowing a little. Was she nervous? "I'm Fen. I was just wondering if you needed any help moving in…"

"Hi." Aria swallowed, trying to push down the slight nausea that suddenly piled at the back of her throat. *It's okay, she's just trying to be friendly. Maybe she's the neighbor across from you.* "I'm Aria. I just…er, I don't need help, but thanks for asking."

Fen offered Aria a soft smile, but it was shaky. "Well, okay. I'm living right across from you so if you need help in navigating the campus or something, let me know."

"Thanks." Aria swallowed. "Er…see you later, I guess."

"See you later!" Fen smiled and turned to leave. Aria took the opportunity to shut the door. However, Aria a bit too fast in doing so, half-slamming it shut. The echoing slam hade Aria's skin crawl, and she pulled her hands away from the doorknob.

"Shit," Aria whispered, just before she heard Aubri groan.

"What was *that* for?" Aria turned to see Aubri frowning as she spoke up. "She was only trying to be nice! I bet she's just as nervous as you."

"I know." A sigh left Aria as she leaned back against the door. "I just...I got tense, and..." She stopped herself, shaking her head. She hated getting all anxious about meeting people - why did interacting with new faces have to feel so *intimidating?* She was excited to be at this school. But learning about this place's history, on top of seeing all the new faces, didn't help her mood. And now she had to live with messing up Fen's first impression of her, too! What if she hated her? What if she thought she was some stuck-up girl that didn't care about others or something?

"I know it's a lot for you." Aubri managed, taking a deep breath, and Aria tried to meet her gaze. Aubri wasn't angry at her – at least, she didn't sound like it. "When Bastian and I first moved in together, we were pretty overwhelmed."

"At least you both knew each other before!" Aria muttered, shaking her head. Her stomach turned as she thought of her encounter with Fen just moments ago. That was bad enough, but what about all the other students in this place!? Her stomach twisted as she forced herself to inhale, then exhale quickly. "I'm just...jumping into this all new. I don't even *know* anyone here!"

"That's true, but…" Aubri paused, before taking a deep breath, looking her in the eye. "Just promise that you won't hide in your room all the time while you're here?"

"I promise." Aria managed, offering her a soft smile. She knew it was a farce, but she wanted to put on a strong front, for Aubri's sake. "I'll try. For you."

"For yourself, too. Not just for me." A soft chuckle left Aubri. "How about we finish unpacking a bit before we go find Bastian and Nick? They're probably looking for us."

"Sounds good." Maybe being around more familiar faces would help lift the mood, get rid of the unease she still felt prickling at her shoulders and twisting her gut.

CHAPTER 6

After a series of texts asking for each others' locations on campus, the group eventually met up again in the campus' main hall. There was a theater on campus, where the welcoming ceremony itself would take place. Everyone took their seats with each other in the area.

The theater itself was huge; the stage wrapped itself around half of the perimeter of the circular theater, creating a large stage for everyone to see. There was no shortage of seats, however; Aubri looked up, as she sat down in her seat, to see that there were two more balconies full of seats for people to enter.

It didn't take long for all the attendees, students, families, and staff alike, to enter the theater and take their seats. The lights dimmed around them, and the stage lit up for Aubri and the others to see who was now there on stage.

"Welcome, students, staff, faculty and families." A woman with dark brown hair and grey eyes addressed the audience. She wore a neat suit jacket over a blouse, and it matched with her dark skirt, stockings, and heels. Aria quietly pointed out to Aubri that this woman was Dr. Stella Reinhart, one of the staff. "It is a pleasure to have all of you here today and welcome to the Da Capo Music Institution. Thank you for coming to this welcoming ceremony. Without further ado, it is my honor to introduce our newest president to give all of you a few words, Dr. Dean Myers!"

The crowd applauded politely, though there was some cheering from the crowd. A man dressed in a black coat, red tie, and white shirt, as well as black trousers and shoes, approached the podium, shaking hands with the vice-president before adjusting the microphone. As the applause died down, he took a deep breath, before speaking.

"Thank you, everyone!" The new president beamed at everyone from where he stood. "It is an honour to be back here at this school not as a former student, but now as its president. Back when I studied here, I made most wonderful memories, honing my craft in music along with my fellow classmates. Being at this academy fostered a deep love and respect for music in me, to share with the rest of the world after graduation."

He took another deep breath, pausing, before continuing with no more hesitation. "I know this school has gone through tremendously hard times, especially in the past year." He continued. "However, as president, I plan to take this school on a reimagined road, working towards a bright and glorious future for this generation of artists, and artists to come. It is the goal of the school to continue the years of musical excellence that blessed this world, and—!"

That was when the acting president coughed, into his hand. He went still, gazing up from his hand and at the audience with a blank look in his eyes, before suddenly keeling over.

Some of the audience screamed as two of the staff members ran up on stage to help the acting president up, but Aubri could see from her seat that the acting president coughed up *blood.* She swallowed, looking away, and she noticed Aria also not watching. Nick stared up at the stage with wide eyes, paling on the spot, and Bastian squeezed his hand, whispering something in his ear before Nick finally looked away.

As Aubri forced herself to look up on the stage, that a medic had come up on stage to assist the two staff members and the acting president.

"He's dead." She overheard one of the staff members mumbling, and all the dread that she held in from watching the man collapse earlier sunk into her stomach, haunting her to the core.

CHAPTER 7

Unlike the last two times, when Aubri was at an isolated beach resort and on a train stuck in the middle of nowhere respectively, the police came within an hour of the acting president's death instead of taking several days. The forensic unit took the body away to be examined, and the concert hall where he died in was cleared out for the police to examine on their own, blocked off by some officers guarding the hall's doors so no one could just waltz in and tamper with the evidence.

Hours later, the acting president was declared dead, and most likely a murder. Poisoning, they said.

While the police investigated the area and barred it off from the public, Aubri, Bastian, Nick, and Aria headed to the cafeteria on campus. It was open today to feed the crowds that came for the welcome/orientation day today. However, with news of the acting president's death emerging, the general atmosphere of the area was much more somber. Aubri felt bad for the new students, and not just Aria. Surely none of them hoped to witness a murder live on stage!

"What do we do?"

The four sat at a table together, away from the other families, staff, and students that spoke about the murder in low voices. She already overheard them reconsidering staying on campus with the killer running amok. She knew it made sense for them to be worried; no one wanted to go to a school if people just kept getting killed there.

"The police are *actually* here this time." Nick managed, swallowing. Aubri looked toward him to see his gaze darting between himself and the others. "Maybe we should just let them handle this."

"What?" Aubri raised a brow. "I'm surprised that you're not suggesting we investigate this. What about your friend, Akeno? He could be in danger."

"Any of us could be in danger." Nick shook his head, frowning. "I told Bastian earlier, but...I saw one of the original murders, about twenty years ago."

"You *what?*" Aubri resisted the urge to drop her jaw, but that wasn't something she expected to hear. "What do you mean by original murders? I thought last year's murders were the only ones!"

Bastian and Nick glanced toward each other briefly,

frowning. A sigh left Nick as he looked toward Aubri and Aria.

"I didn't want to have to tell you two, but I was on a school trip with my class to this place twenty years ago. What we didn't know was that there was a murderer on the loose at the time. I got lost during the tour, and I witnessed one of the other students dying at the time. Of course," He shook his head briefly, "No one believed me at first. And even after the murderer was uncovered, the school paid a massive amount of hush money to cover up those murders."

"Is that why we only know about the ones from last year?" Aria frowned.

"Probably. And honestly," Nick's nose wrinkled at that, "I don't want to be involved in this case if I don't have to."

Aubri swallowed. She wanted to snap at Nick for not telling her and Aria sooner about all of this. But at the same time, she could guess why he didn't want to talk about it. It was like how she hated anyone bringing up her past with Renee from the beach resort at this point. It just wasn't a subject that she really wanted to approach again if she didn't have to.

"If that's what you want, then you don't have to." Aria spoke, after a moment. Aubri glanced toward her to see her frowning. "I'm sorry you went through all of that. If I'd known, I wouldn't have asked you to help me move in."

"Don't apologize. I'm just sorry for not mentioning this earlier." Nick shook his head, before his gaze snapped toward Aria. "I know I feel like I should back out of this one, but at the same time, I feel like I *have* to be involved in this. Like you said, Akeno is possibly in danger. I know he was, from last year's murders. But I can't just investigate this alone – I wouldn't get far that way."

"You won't be alone. Not like what you went through last time." Bastian put a hand on his shoulder, squeezing it gently. "I want to help with this, too."

"Well," Aubri looked between Bastian and Nick, and then looked towards Aria, "I'm not about to let any of you get hurt while you're here. Count me in."

Aria offered her a sheepish grin. "I don't think I can just withdraw from the school immediately. Maybe I can withdraw from the courses themselves and take the term off if you're worried about my safety, but…"

"It's not fair that you should have to do that, though!" Aubri muttered, shaking her head. "What are the other students going to do? Hole up in hotels close to the school so they don't have to stay on-campus while the killer's lurking around?"

"Some might." Aria admitted, biting her lower lip briefly. "I overheard a few students talking to each other about that while we vacated the theater earlier."

"Well, we won't get anything solved off-campus." Bastian pointed out. "And this is, what, the third murder we've come across personally?"

"Fourth for me." Nick muttered, shrugging. "Counting the one from that twenty-something years ago, that is."

"Either way, we have experience on our side this time." Bastian managed, trying to meet Nick's gaze. "Nick, I'm sure there will be students trying to stick together in groups on campus. Aria should probably do the same." He looked towards Aria, frowning. "Do you...know anyone on campus, yet? Made any friends?"

Aria swallowed, glancing around before speaking. "Er... I know someone from across my room. Her name was Fen, I think? I guess I could ask her if she could stick with me outside of classes, but I don't know."

"Better than nothing." Aubri interjected. At least, she hoped that it was better than nothing. Maybe Fen even knew something about this school's past. If not her, though, who else could they ask for help and information?

"What about you, though?" Aria frowned as she looked between Bastian, Nice, and Aubri. "All of you don't live close to campus."

"I work remotely." Aubri was glad that she had a flexible job right now. "I'll be fine with an internet connection anywhere! I could book a hotel room with Bastian and Nick to share or get my own."

"Probably for the best. Besides, I have the week off work, and so does Nick." Bastian managed, but then he looked at Aria. "You could room with us off-campus, if you're worried for your own safety."

Aria shook her head. "I might be able to find things out as a student on campus, so it might be best for me to stay here if I can. If I'm not completely alone, I should be okay...but...will anyone be willing to help me with any of this? What about the other students' safety?"

"I'm sure the staff are trained in self-defence since at least last year's murders." Nick frowned. "Bastian, you left me and Akeno before he told me this, but he had to go through mandatory training when he got hired as a TA. The same probably goes for anyone else at least recently hired."

"It's not the lack of self-defence that I'm worried about."

Aria managed, shaking her head. "If we're investigating this case, the staff will likely keep the details of what the police found out hush-hush. How are we supposed to persuade them to let us help them find out who the killer is?"

Aria had a good point. It wasn't like anyone had any super-close connections at this school. Aubri knew that Nick and Akeno were friends, but Akeno was only a TA. She noticed Bastian's eyes light up before he snapped his fingers.

"Why don't we ask Louise?" Bastian suddenly spoke up. "She might know a thing or two about this whole campus and its staff. She probably has some idea of what the police found out so far, about the murder."

Aria stared up at Bastian. "Louise?" She repeated, and Aubri frowned at hearing the name. It sounded strangely familiar, but she wasn't entirely sure who it belonged to.

"You know her better as Lulu, Aria, one of the women who your late father – my brother – had an affair with." Bastian clarified, swallowing lightly. "She's working here under her real name now. I saw her earlier, before we met up to watch the opening ceremonies."

"What?" Aubri's jaw dropped. Out of everyone Aubri expected to potentially see again, since the whole murder mystery on the train, it was her? "She's *here?*"

"Apparently someone 'anonymously' recommended her for the job. She thought it was me, but…I haven't talked to her at all since the engagement party." Bastian shook his head a little. "I don't know who did it. But whoever did recommend her helped her get a job working here as an admin. She might know a thing or two about this campus' history and the current situation."

"Let's finish eating before we talk to her, first." Nick managed. "I think it's a case better handled if we don't have empty stomachs."

CHAPTER 8

The group found Louise Anders' office with little trouble. Bastian knocked on the door, before walking in.

"Oh, it's you." Louise sighed as she looked up at them from where she sat, putting down the papers on her desk. Her hair from earlier was messier than when Bastian last saw her, eyes struggling to focus on him and the others. "Let me guess: You want to investigate this case?"

"Yup." Bastian managed, looking her in the eye. He offered her a soft grin. "*And* I think you can help us."

Her nose wrinkled at his statement. "I'm surprised you're not running to the vice president or one of the higher ups about this. Why ask me, of all people? Or, I don't know, why can't you just leave this to the police?"

"To answer your first question, it's because you're the one that's most likely going to help us, out of everyone here." Bastian explained, frowning. "We have our history on that train together, and I can trust you. Everyone else here is a stranger to us – most people, at least. As for your second question, I doubt most of the school staff would *willingly* give us information to investigate this compared to the police – nor would the police want us to help since we're civilians."

"Your answers make some sense at least. You *did* solve that crime before any of the train's security did, too." She got up from behind her desk, moving to stand around it. "Alright, I'll tell you what I know. Shoot your questions now, or forever hold your peace."

Bastian looked towards Aubri, who spoke up first. "What do you know about the acting president's murder?"

"Really cutting straight to the chase, aren't you?" Louise pushed a few strands of hair out of her face, lips twisting lightly before she answered. "He overdosed. The police figured that someone must've drugged his drink right before his speech – Dean Myers has no history of drug or alcohol abuse, as far as I know. The police are still investigating the cafeteria and the leftover food served from the welcome event earlier this morning to see if any of that got tainted with drugs, so I don't know what type of drug he got poisoned with. Whatever it was, it was enough to be lethal."

At least they somewhat knew the cause of death, Bastian supposed. "Did they talk about any possible suspects?"

She shook her head. "None yet. But I overheard a couple of the staff say it mirrored a death from last year, when a student was secretly drugged without them knowing and then died of an overdose an hour later." She visibly shuddered at that. "That's a terrible way to go."

"True..." Bastian looked towards Nick. He already looked pale, wrapping his arms around himself, clearly trying to keep his composure. Bastian offered him his hand, his eyes meeting the other's own. Nick almost instantly grabbed his hand, squeezing it and mouthing 'thanks' back to him.

"Copycat killer, maybe?" Aria frowned, brows furrowing. "But why?"

"Maybe they idolized the original killer." Aubri mused. She noticed her sister visibly shudder at the statement, but she pressed on. "Or it could be a way of experimenting with how they like to kill people best. Alternatively, assuming the new president was supposed to be the only target, they figured overdosing was the easiest way to take him out, and the mirroring is a coincidence from last year."

Louise frowned, shaking her head as she adjusted her glasses. "One of the students that personally witnessed the president die *is* on-campus in her second year, right now. Her name's Fen Zheng. You can probably find her at the old church on-campus, since that's where all the students in the Pipe Organ program go for their one-on-one sessions. You'll likely run into her instructor, Astlyr Anderson, as well."

"Why would Fen be at the church?" Aubri tilted her head to the side.

"It's one of the few places where pipe organs are available on campus." Louis managed, a sheepish grin appearing on her face. "The Pipe Organ program is the smallest one in the entire school. All the students in that program take turns accompanying church services to gain practical experience working, so they often practice directly at the church before each service. Fen is likely there, if not at her dorm room like the other students."

"Sorry, you said...Fen, right?" Aria's brows furrowed before a gasp left her. "I remember her! She was the one that introduced herself when Aubri and I moved my things into my dorm room earlier."

Wasn't that convenient, Bastian couldn't help but think before speaking up. "I guess we know what Fen looks like already, but what about Astlyr? What does he look like?"

"Astlyr's older, blond, paler skin. There aren't any new pipe organ students that enrolled this year, so Fen's the youngest of the students. Shouldn't be hard to miss. However," Louise frowned, shaking her head. "The poor girl's super-skittish from all those murders. If you're approaching her, you should be careful not to scare her. She's gone through a lot from last year."

Aubri bit the inside of her cheek briefly. "Thanks…Is there anyone else that was heavily involved in the cases from last year, that's also on campus?"

"Well…" Louise paused, then sighed. "Akeno Botan, and Ashanti Owusu were also both involved in the previous case as students – apparently, both them and Fen personally investigated the murders, both actual and attempted, of the other students and staff."

"They did?" Nick frowned lightly, and Bastian noticed the other mutter under his breath, a bit softer, "Is that why Akeno said he didn't want to talk much about it earlier…?"

"There was a case of one other student, Meghan Ishikawa, who survived her murder attempt thanks to other students saving her life. However," Louise continued, adjusted her glasses with a sigh, "Meghan's taking this term off, so she's not on campus right now and is back at her hometown. Since she had a clear alibi and isn't even on this campus, the police already ruled her out as a suspect."

"What about Ashanti Owusu?" Aubri asked.

Louise shook her head. "The same goes for Ms. Owusu as well. She's taking this term off, so she wasn't on campus to begin with." Her eyes flashed slightly as she picked up a file, reading through it. "All the other students that were targeted last year were successfully killed. I *could* contact Ms. Ishikawa and Owusu and ask if they could have a phone interview with one of you if you want to ask them about last year's murders. But I don't know how well that would go. Plus, they'd need to give consent before I can give you their contact information, for privacy reasons."

"Since both aren't even on campus and therefore dead ends, there's no point." Bastian frowned. He, Aubri, Aria, and Nick all knew at this point that investigating any murder mystery just kept leaving some sort of scar – one they'd rather not talk too much about.

"What about Akeno? He told me he was involved in the cases last year." Nick frowned. "What about any other staff – could we try talking to them? Were there any specific professors, faculty, and so on that tried intervening with the murders?"

"All of the staff tried their best to put in preventative measures, but there were two that were almost murdered in the process." Louise answered. "Dixie La Bisette and Astlyr Anderson. Dixie was stabbed but survived thanks to Maximus

Crispin finding her injured and getting her medical help in time. Astlyr Anderson was almost pushed off the roof but was rescued before he could be harmed. His attempted murder was also the same night that the previous president died."

Aubri tried not to imagine falling off the roof as Louise mentioned it, but Renee's final screams echoed in her mind. She shook her head lightly, doing her best to ignore it, before speaking up again. "Do you have any idea where Akeno might be? Or Professors La Bisette and Crispin?" The sooner she and the others got to them, the sooner they could find out more information.

"Well, Akeno is likely having office hours right now." Louise managed. "After all, he is TA. I can write down his room number for you, and it's close to the practice rooms in this building. Bisette is probably at her office, and I'll write down her room and phone numbers for you too. Her office is pretty close to Crispin's, but I'll write down his room and phone numbers as well."

Bastian looked towards Nick. "Do you want to find Akeno and talk to him?"

"I was thinking that I could find Dixie, Maximus and Astlyr, actually." Nick managed. "I trust that you and Akeno will get along."

Bastian nodded. "I'll find him, then."

"If that's the case," Aubri managed, "Aria, how about you get settled into your dorm room? I can go find Fen at the church. I saw it on the way into the main building, when I first entered the campus, so I think I know my way from there."

"Okay." Aria took a deep breath, looking her sister in the eye. "Be careful out there, okay? Text me or one of us if you're in trouble."

"I will. Same goes for you."

"Of course."

The group turned to leave, but Bastian looked towards Louise, taking a deep breath. "Lulu? Thanks for your help. Stay safe, okay?"

Aubri noticed her smile lightly at Bastian. "Thanks. You stay alive, too. For all our sakes."

CHAPTER 9

Aubri could already hear music as she approached the church alone. She guessed that Fen Zheng had to be in there. Aubri remembered Louise telling her and the others about Fen and her involvement in last year's murders. Of course, Fen survived, or else Aubri wouldn't be able to talk to her today.

Aubri couldn't help but wonder, as she pushed open the wooden doors and walked into the church, how to approach the subject of the acting president's murder with her. If Fen was as skittish as Louise described, it could be difficult. The way she described Fen reminded Aubri of when she first met Aria. Her sister had her own anxiety with being around people, and she didn't like talking about murder. Maybe Fen was similar.

The church's pipe organ reverberated through the whole building, greeting Aubri with deep, low notes. The sounds reminded her of attending church services when she was younger, with the organist up in the balcony above. However, the music piece itself was unfamiliar to her.

If someone was playing the pipe organ, and the organ

wasn't in the main sanctuary, was it, and its musician playing it, on the floor above her? Aubri looked to her left, then right, before heading left after noticing a stairway. Slowly and silently making her way up the steps, she listened to the music on the entire way there. It was inviting, despite its unfamiliarity, and chimes sounded briefly as she nearly reached the next floor.

At the top of the steps, entering the second floor, she saw a familiar young woman with dark hair sitting at the pipe organ. This was definitely Fen, based on what Aubri recalled from when she and Aria first saw her. It was hard to tell what Fen's whole figure looked like from where Aubri stood, given that Aubri could only see her head from the second-floor entrance. Fen had a concentrated look on her face complete with furrowed brows and a hard gaze. If Aubri hadn't known Fen was a student here, she would assume that the other was a teenager, given her youthful, rounded face.

The music ended. Fen sighed, leaning back slightly where she sat, and Aubri used the opportunity to speak up, taking a step toward her.

"Excuse me? Fen? I'm Aubri, from earlier – can I speak with you for a moment?"

Fen slammed her hands onto the keyboard, a gasp tearing from her lips. A cacophonous chorus wailed from the pipes. Aubri covered her ears at the horrid mixture of sound, grimacing.

"Shit!" She looked up as the sour-sounding chords faded. The pipe-organist swallowed, moving to get off the bench to properly face Aubri with a sheepish grimace. "I'm sorry, I didn't notice you. I really didn't mean it, I *swear!*"

"It's no problem." Aubri reassured her, offering her a reassuring grin. "Lost in the music, I guess?"

"Yeah…y-yeah." Fen pushed a few strands of dark hair out of her face, making the sign of one cross and mouthing *Forgive me Father for swearing,* before looking up at Aubri. "Sorry, but can I get your name? I don't think we've met before. Or did we? Wait." Her brows furrowed, leaning forwards, and squinting a bit. "Aria? Is that you?"

"I think you mistook me for my twin sister." Aubri clarified quickly. "I'm Aubri Harlow. Sorry about Aria slamming the door in your face earlier, by the way – she's not the greatest with people, but she's working on it."

"Oh." Fen nodded a bit, offering her a sheepish grin. "Sorry about that. And no worries, I understand – I'm not great with people, either. I think I did the same thing in my first year, too." A soft chuckle left her at that. Aubri wasn't sure whether she was just still nervous and trying to hide it, based on how forced it sounded.

"One of the staff told me that you took part in investigating last year's murders. Do you mind if we talk about that, right now?"

"Me? I…" Fen took a deep breath, before a sigh left her lips, shaking her head slightly. "Er…feel free to sit on one of the pews. I think this will be a long story."

Aubri moved to sit down on one of the wooden pews, and Fen sat beside her.

"I know that what happened in the past year might be uncomfortable for you to talk about." Aubri explained, "But I have a feeling that this might be attached to the acting president's death. This isn't the first time that murder happened on campus, after all."

"That's true." Fen admitted. "About twenty years ago, there was a series of murders. Of course, no one found out who did it back then. And last year, the killer tried to kill me, *and* my friends. She even succeeded in killing several of the students last year, killed the previous president, and so on." Fen visibly shuddered, biting her own lip. "It was horrible. I just…when the acting president came up dead just the other day, it wasn't fair.

Why did this have to happen all over *again?*"

All over again? Aubri frowned. "The acting president's death wasn't the first one you witnessed?" She knew that Louise told her earlier that Fen witnessed the previous president die, but had she seen any other deaths?

"No. I've seen my friends die, or at least their corpses being carried out of the school. It's…" She shook her head. "It's not something you want to see. I didn't think that *anyone* would die here." She swallowed, averting her gaze from Aubri. "One of my roommates, Joanna, suddenly disappeared once. We all just thought that she ditched school after the pressure got to her – and I've heard of people dropping out, out of frustration. A week later, we found out that her corpse was stuffed in a spare piece of luggage and left on the train leaving campus for the train's staff to discover later, after it was already enroute elsewhere."

Aubri couldn't stop herself from visualizing it. She'd seen too many corpses at this point in her life, and it made things too easy to see in her mind's eye these days. If she didn't keep asking about the past murders, however, how else would she find out the killer's motive? "Do you have any idea why the past killer killed the students in the first place?"

Fen looked up at her, nodding. "She was a copycat of a past killer – at least, that's the theory my friend Ashanti came up with. Twenty years ago, there was another student who killed her own fellow classmates and even fellow staff members because she was jealous of their artistic and musical abilities. Last year's killer wanted to do something similar, to destroy the next generation of geniuses so she can have the reputation of the most innovative one of all because she thought they were *too* good to graduate – at least, that's what she said at the time. It's *sick.*" She swallowed, paling. "What if…whoever killed the acting president is continuing her work? Or copying the copycat? How many more of us are going to *die* because of that?"

Aubri thought of Aria, and how excited she was to join this school. She'd talked about it for *months* after receiving the acceptance letter, and Aubri thought that Aria might have what it takes to make it in music.

Does that mean this current killer is a copycat of a copycat? That's fucked up.

For Aria, and other people just as excited as her to attend this school, only to meet their demises – that wasn't fair to her, or any of the students that suffered last year like Fen did. She resisted the urge to grit her teeth, looking Fen in the eye before speaking up.

"My friends and I are going to find out who killed the acting president." Aubri told her. "We've solved crimes like this before. In the meantime, it's best if you stick with a friend or two when you can. And not just during class, either."

"That's hard." Fen grimaced. "I don't know if you know, but learning pipe organ is often a solitary activity, even if you're with an instructor for private lessons."

Aubri tried to offer her a smile. It was the best she could do. "Bring a friend to listen in, then. They might like it. Maybe you'll even convince them to join the program afterwards!"

Fen laughed, her voice soft, but at least she had a smile on her face this time. "You think so?"

"Yeah. I mean," Aubri shrugged, "I don't really how you manage to play this huge instrument, but you sounded good when I heard you playing, earlier."

"Really? Thanks." Fen seemed a little calmer now since they weren't talking about death and murder for the moment. "I was practicing an Intermezzo from "Cavalleria Rusticana" by Pietro Mascagni. It's originally from an opera, but this piece is a pipe organ arrangement."

"*Cavalleria?*" Aubri's nose scrunched up slightly as she tried to pronounce the name. "I don't think I know that one too well."

"It's okay. Not a lot of people know that one." She paused,

moving to take a music book off the pipe organ's stand. "I was finishing up practicing, so…if you don't mind," Her face flushed lightly, "Maybe you can accompany me back to the dorm building? For safety?"

"Sure." Aubri paused, frowning. "You mentioned Ashanti just earlier. She investigated last year's murders, right? Can you tell me more about her?"

Fen nodded. "She lived in the room across from mine when last year's murders happened. She also personally investigated those deaths, and I helped…kind-of." Fen shuddered at that. "I was worried for her, back then. In a way, I'm glad she's not on campus right now. She seriously needed a break after all that happened." Aubri noticed her wrap her arms tight around herself as she kept talking. "I should have helped more. Maybe she wouldn't be so hurt if…"

"I'm sure she's just happy that you're still alive after all of that happened." Aubri tried to reassure her. "How about we head to the dorm together?"

Fen nodded. "Of course. Just follow me!"

As Aubri and Fen left the church together, Aubri took one last look at the church before continuing on her way to the dorms. She had a feeling this would be a good place to hide from a killer…or a good place to find a body. She wasn't sure which one was more likely.

"My question is," Aubri managed, as they continued walking on the way to the dorms "Why did you come back to this school, then, if you didn't want to see more death? Because you thought things were fine now, or…?"

Fen swallowed. "Well, this school *does* have some of the best music programs. Even if there was death, there are still people here that I trust and want to be with, as well as learn from them. I thought that if I stayed…maybe I might make some better memories than last time. Now, I'm not so sure."

"I'm sorry to hear that." Aubri swallowed lightly. "I just hope that we can finish this case before more victims emerge."

She heard Fen sigh. "I hope so, too."

Aubri could tell, looking at Fen's forlorn eyes, that her hopes dwindled quickly.

CHAPTER 10

Bastian wished he didn't have to be the one talking to Akeno. It was awkward enough for him, knowing that this was one of Nick's closest friends he was speaking to. It didn't help that they only just met on the day of the murder either. However, Nick was busy finding the other staff to talk with, so Bastian figured that *someone* had to do it.

Bastian knocked on the open door to Akeno's office, before speaking up. "Akeno? May I speak with you?"

Akeno's head snapped upwards, looking towards Bastian, before visibly relaxing, sinking slightly into his chair. "Depends on what it's about, I'm afraid." He managed, pushing a few strands of hair behind his ear. "Wasn't expecting to hear from you."

"It'll be quick, I promise." Bastian closed the door behind him, before looking the younger man in the eye. "I have a few questions about the previous murders you witnessed. You were present, last year, when the students were being murdered. That's what Louise told me earlier. I thought…"

Akeno tensed, a grimace overtaking his face. "Does this have to do with the most recent murder?" He asked.

"It *might*." Bastian admitted, biting the inside of his cheek briefly before continuing. "My friends and I are looking into it. Aubri's talking to Fen, Aria's settling into her dorm room, and Nick is trying to ask some of the faculty and staff for further information."

Akeno raised a brow, shaking his head. "And you're not leaving this investigation to the police? Why?"

"As far as I heard from Louise, the police weren't helpful the last time murders happened here." Bastian managed, sighing. And in his and Aubri's cases with the past two murders they investigated, there were virtually no police available to help to begin with! "I also wanted to ask about when you and Nick witnessed one of the first murders, over twenty years ago, because it sounds like it's potentially connected to these new murders, too. If you don't mind."

Akeno frowned, and Bastian saw that the younger man looked like he struggled with what to say. His eyes strained to reach a conclusion, before he sighed, closing his eyes.

"I have little choice but to tell you more details." Akeno opened his eyes again, looking up to meet Bastian's gaze. "Nick and I were in elementary school at the time, when we were here on a field trip. We got lost when we wandered away from the other students, and we hid when we saw one of the victims get murdered. Neither of us saw exactly who the killer was, or why they did it at the time. Flash forward to last year, and a classmate who idolized that past killer tried killing me and several other fellow students – and even killed the president." He shuddered, shaking his head. "Do you and the others seriously think that they're all connected to this one?"

"Yeah. Aubri came up with the idea. She's got a knack for murder mysteries at this point." Bastian admitted. He could see Akeno's shoulders tense, but Bastian kept talking. "But if that's the case, someone's carrying on or copying the previous killer's work…and has the same or similar motivation, to do so. Do you know any potential classmates that would be jealous enough to kill anyone? I know the world of music can be…competitive."

Like my own family, Bastian wanted to add, but he refrained from doing so. His own brother was already dead, after all, and he just got his meddlesome father out of his life for good not long ago.

"It's true that studying music is competitive, but same goes for any area of the arts." Akeno frowned, leaning back in his chair. His brows furrowed, and he closed his eyes briefly. "If there's anyone jealous enough to kill the new acting president, it's one of the staff members. I don't know all of the newly hired staff too well, but it could be one of the ones still alive and present from last year. Another idea I have is..." He adjusted his reading glasses. "I know that Astlyr Anderson applied for the position of president after the old one died, but he dropped out of the running before the interviews even began."

"Astlyr Anderson?" Bastian remembered Louise telling him about that man. "He's the head of the Pipe Organ program, correct?"

"Yes, him." The younger man nodded once.

That was the second time Bastian heard his name, at this point. "I should speak with him. Is there anyone else you can think of? Anyone else that you know that tried to be the acting president, or didn't work well with Mr. Myers?"

Akeno shook his head. "No. That's all I know."

Bastian had a feeling he wouldn't find out much more from Akeno – though what he did learn was useful. "Thank you for your time. I should find Astlyr. Do you have any idea where he might be, now?"

The other frowned. "He's likely out to lunch. He always goes out with Dixie La Bisette and Maximus Crispin."

"Dixie? Maximus?" Bastian didn't know those names for sure. *And who the hell names their children Dixie and Maximus?*

"They're instructors from the Piano program." Akeno explained, raising a brow. "T hose two wear elaborate fashion pieces, so it shouldn't be hard to miss them."

"I see." Bastian wondered how extravagant Dixie and Maximus dressed, but he supposed he'd find out once he met them. Hopefully Astlyr wasn't dressed as fancily as those two were. "Well, thank you. I'll make sure to keep an eye out."

As he turned to leave, he heard Akeno call out, "Wait. There's one more thing I need to tell you."

Bastian turned, faced him. Worry cracked through Akeno's otherwise stoic face, particularly in his eyes. "Yes?"

"Keep Nick safe, okay?" Akeno asked, swallowing. "I'm glad that you're happy together. Drawing off from what I experienced last year, however, he could be in *serious* danger if he's not careful. Same goes for you and the others with you."

"We'll be careful." A sigh left Bastian. "This is literally the third murder case I've helped investigate, so I think we have a little more experience than the last two times to handle that. But we'll still be careful regardless."

Akeno nodded once, a weary sigh leaving him. "Good

luck. You'll need it."

Bastian nodded, before turning to leave Akeno's office. "I know I will." He just hoped that Akeno wouldn't become a victim of the new murderer haunting this school – or anyone else, too soon.

CHAPTER 11

Aria took a deep breath as she made it to her dorm room, checking in there to see if there was any killer. After all, who knows? What if the person who killed the new president was a student, and not a staff member?

Then again, she supposed that didn't make the most sense.

Things would eventually be fine, right? All she had to do was make sure she didn't slam the door in her face like she did to Fen. She didn't want to gain a reputation as someone who slammed doors in people's faces. That never ended well, and she didn't want to make enemies out of anyone at a competitive school – let alone one known for several murders.

She glanced towards the violin case in her room – she hadn't touched it at all since she arrived at the school, since moving in. Her hands shook at her sides, and she knew deep down that playing a bit would help ease her nerves – but would it also attract a killer?

She would keep her door locked, she guessed. Windows, too. It wouldn't be too hard to muffle the room either. She put her blanket up against the window and pushed her mattress up against the door. The benefits of having a single room to herself meant that she could make it as soundproof as she pleased. She knew she should be helping investigate a murder, potentially more than one if the killer was lurking around. But she also needed space and time to process and stay safe. Surely a short break from investigating wouldn't hurt.

She took the violin and bow out of their case before applying the rosin to the bow. It had been a while since she last played violin – at least over a day. Ever since the events of the murder on the train, she found herself throwing herself into music more – partially to get into this school, and partially because it was a solace. When she was playing music, she didn't have to think of anything else.

And now here she was, stuck in a music school where a murder just happened – her dream and nightmare turned into one. A sigh left her as she moved the violin to rest on her shoulder, under her chin, before lifting the bow towards the strings and beginning to play.

It was a somber tune, this piece – *Pavane, Opus 50 by Fauré*, she reminded herself. It was her audition piece for getting into this school, but the more she practiced it, the more she enjoyed it. The strings vibrated as their sounds reverberated through the room, despite Aria's best attempts to muffle the room itself. She didn't mind, though – it made her think less, and just focus on the music. Despite the mournful tune, it was a comfort to her right now – one she needed right now.

A knock at the door suddenly jolted her out of the music, made her pause. Should she answer? It would be rude not to, wouldn't it?

But what if it was the killer? Aria's stomach curled into knots as she put her violin and bow back in their case. What if she was the next victim? What then? She first pushed the mattress out of the way of the door, before she reached for a binder on her music stand – perhaps not the best weapon to defend herself, but better than nothing. With her free hand, she took a deep breath before opening the door.

At the door, Aria found a note attached to it. She paused, glancing around – whoever was in the hall earlier to leave the note there was gone. She opened it up, reading:

Want to know more info? I can provide that. Meet me on the roof in five minutes.

No signature. Aria's guts twisted. Was it a good idea to

go up there alone? All by herself? What would Aubri do in a situation like this? Aria closed the door, putting the note in her pocket and taking out her phone. Should she go up there by herself, or wait for Aubri?

Then again, the note seemed urgent. Maybe…

She paused, before taking out her phone and texting Aubri. *Someone wants to talk to me on the roof. Should I go?*

How soon? Aubri texted back.

Like, now.

I'm enroute to your dorm building. Don't go up there alone.

Aria swallowed, before texting. *Okay, I'll –*

That was when she heard the screaming. Aria stopped, before rushing to the window and pulling the blinds open –

Just in time to see a body hit the ground outside of the school building.

She gagged, looking away, before hurriedly texting Aubri. Her shaky hands made more spelling mistakes than she hoped for, but she knew that she had to tell her. Eventually she sent the message – and then immediately called campus police after.

CHAPTER 12

Aubri was fast to get to Aria as soon as she saw the message – and Fen came along, too. By the time they arrived, there were campus police setting up a crime scene around a spot outside the dorm building. Several students, staff, and other onlookers tried to crowd around the scene, forcing the police to ward them off.

Aubri knew that the corpse wasn't Aria – but what if it *had* been? The sight of the crowd, the dead body, and the police only prompted her to run faster. Who died this time? Why *now?*

"Aubri, wait!" It was Fen calling, but Aubri barely heeded her words as she ran into the building, then up the first set of stairs. Fen panted for breath, running a pace or two behind her, but Aubri didn't care – who she was more worried about was Aria herself.

"Aria!" Aubri heard herself yell. "Aria, are you okay!?"

"Aubri!?"

Aubri turned, just in time, to see Aria rush over to her.

Both sisters wrapped each other in tight embraces.

"I was worried," Aubri gasped, hugging her close, and she felt Aria's arms tighten around her.

"I-I followed your instructions; I didn't leave my room." Aria shook her head. "I-I heard the body..."

"Damn." Aubri pulled back a bit to see Aria's face. Her twin sister's eyes were slightly reddened, and she struggled to hold it together. "Did you already talk to the police...?"

"I-I already did. They said they'll handle the rest. I think whoever was killed was pushed off the roof. A-apparently," Aria hugged Aubri close again as she lowered her voice to a whisper, "She got a note, too, luring her to the balcony..."

"Oh god." Aubri's stomach twisted. Didn't Louise mention that last year's president was pushed off the balcony by that same year's killer? She took a deep breath, looking Aria in the eye. "I don't want you staying on campus overnight, okay? We need to get you out of here for tonight."

"But what if something else happens on campus while we're gone?" Aria breathed.

Aubri shook her head. "I don't want to risk your safety, or the others." She rasped. "You could've died if you went up there just earlier, and I'm not taking a risk a second time."

"Okay." Aria forced herself to take a deep breath, and both sisters let go of each other. "What do we do, then?"

"We need to get back to Bastian and Nick. Let them know what's up." Aubri took out her phone, before noticing that there was a new notification. "What the...?"

"What is it?"

"It's Nick." Aubri felt her blood run cold. "Someone else died. *Just now.*"

CHAPTER 13

Nick wasn't sure what to expect when asking the other staff. Louise was the easiest to talk to, though, that was for sure.

Everyone else he'd asked kept their mouths shut or assured him that the police were working on the case, and he shouldn't worry about it. But was that really the case? Or were they trying to sweep this death under the rug, while trying to figure out what to do with no acting president in the picture for their school, now?

Nick knew that he had to speak to some of the staff, but many were too busy and occupied with teaching students or making sure they were safe. At least they were doing their jobs, he supposed.

As he turned the corner while walking down the school halls, passing by students and staff that were whispering to each other about the recent murder, he noticed two people. One was an older man, dressed in a long coat with matching trousers and black shoes. The man pushed a few strands of silvering hair out of his face, but Nick was sure the man needed to comb out his hair or straighten it (or both) before he could get it nice and neat.

The other was a woman who looked around the same age as the man currently sitting in a wheelchair and wearing an elaborate, ruffled blue dress. Were they teachers? Nick knew that he had to take a chance, and he approached them, clearing his throat to get their attention.

"Excuse me?" He spoke up, and both turned their heads to face him. "My name's Nick, and I'm a friend of one of the other students here. I was wondering if I could ask either of you about the murders from, uh…last year?"

Both Maximus and Dixie froze at the statement, and Nick wondered what they were thinking – were their reactions one of fear, from recalling the events of last year?

"What is it exactly that you want to talk to us about?" Dixie's mouth became a thin line, brows furrowing. "If you plan on playing amateur sleuth like some of the other students did, I suggest you leave it up to campus security and the police."

"Dixie," Maximus started, brows furrowing and a frown settling on his face as he looked towards her, "I'm sure he means well. And considering how *useless* the police were last year, maybe he'll be of some help."

The way he called the police useless made Nick swallow. Why was it that in so many of the murder mysteries he found himself caught up in, the police were useless most of the time? Why did it always have to fall to him, Bastian, and the others to solve it all? It wasn't fair!

"Do you think there's a connection between this year's murders and last year's?" Dixie spoke, still eyeing Nick with clear suspicion.

"Er, yeah, actually." Nick admitted – it felt best to tell the truth. With how tense Dixie and Maximus appeared to be, he doubted that they were the killers themselves. "That's one theory that I've heard. I just figured, you know, the school's got a bloodstained history. And I know that last year's murders weren't the only ones that happened here."

"What do you mean, not the only ones?" The man frowned. "Are you referring to the murders from twenty years ago?"

This might be his chance to get them to listen to him – and Nick knew, despite the pain, that it might be worth telling them to do so. "Yeah. Because I was there when one of them happened. I was a schoolkid – on a field trip here, and I hid with another fellow student when we saw someone get murdered."

"Ah…" The man frowned, looking towards Nick. "I see. Now that I think about it, I do recognize you. You're Nick, aren't you?"

Nick frowned. "You actually remember me?" He remembered running to a few staff members with Akeno after they both witnessed the one murder in hiding. "Sorry, I don't."

"I'm not surprised that you don't remember me." The other man quipped, a light smile appearing on his face. "I've changed my wardrobe significantly since then. But…" A frown replaced the smile, "Despite all these years, I sometimes still see the scared boys from that day."

Nick's stomach turned. Maximus kept speaking, a wistful look appearing in his eyes. "I still remember seeing you two. You were both so shocked that you could barely speak to anyone outside of the police and your teachers. I'd only just started teaching at the academy at the time, so I wasn't sure what to do…"

Before Maximus could say any more, a phone suddenly rang. Nick instinctively checked his own pockets for his cellphone, then realized it wasn't ringing. He then looked up to see Dixie taking her phone out, frowning.

"Excuse me," Dixie managed, holding up her cellphone

briefly. "I need to take this call in my office. Seems important."

With that, she moved her wheelchair down the hall, and Nick watched her go before she turned a corner and vanished. He heard Maximus sigh, and he looked towards him, noticing the soft frown on his face, lines appearing on his forehead.

"It's probably something from her doctor." Maximus explained, but Nick noticed him bite his lower lip briefly before continuing. "She...hasn't been the same since the murder attempt on her life."

"Is that..." Nick looked towards the direction Dixie went in, and then towards him, "That's the reason why she's in a wheelchair now, right?"

Maximus' nose scrunched up, but he nodded. "Yeah. Last year's killer *literally* stabbed her in the back. Hit some nerves and other spots that affected her mobility. It's a miracle she survived." A sigh left the other again. "I found her, bleeding out. If I hadn't gotten help in time...I'm not sure if she would even be alive."

Nick recalled how Renee tried killing him and Bastian, back at the beach resort. What if both got shot in the spine or somewhere that affected their limbs? Would they be able to move like they could now, or would they be wheelchair-bound like Dixie? "How is she now?"

He shrugged. "Better. She tries to smile more, but I know a lot of it is fake. I can tell by her eyes – she never fully looks someone in the eyes if she's smiling insincerely."

Nick tried to offer him a reassuring smile. "Sounds like you know her really well. Bet she's happy to have you around."

"Well, we do. We've known each other since our days as students in this school, actually." A light smile came to Maximus' face. "It was a dream come true for both of us to teach here together, but now..." His smile faded, and he shook his head. "I might consider leaving if all these deaths are just going to continue. It's not worth it, you know?"

"Yeah." Nick swallowed lightly. He'd left his job after the whole massacre incident, back at the beach resort. And he almost considered quitting his bartending job after the events on the train, but he'd stuck with it this time. "I think I understand."

He noticed Maximus look down the hallway where Dixie went, frowning. "Dixie's taking a while. I mean, don't get me wrong; I know she usually has her calls, but...this is taking longer than usual."

Nick frowned. Were most of her phone calls usually brief?

"Do you think it's serious news?" He asked. "You said that she was paralyzed below the waist for life – maybe it's a medical-related call?"

The other man shrugged. "Maybe. Maybe not. Who knows?"

Nick felt his stomach twist. What if the killer saw Dixie alone? "Maybe we should go check on her and see if she's okay." He suggested quickly. "I mean, I still want to ask her questions as well, so…"

Maximus nodded quickly. "Of course – I know the way to her office. Please, follow me."

Nick accompanied Maximus to Dr. Bisette's office, and he expected to overhear Dr. Bisette speaking into her cellphone from inside the office, or maybe some shuffling of papers. Instead, there was silence.

Something didn't feel right about this.

"Dr. Bisette?" Nick knocked on the office door. "Is everything okay? Dr. Crispin and I just thought we'd check in on you."

There was no response. He took a step towards the door,

wondering if he could maybe eavesdrop and hear her...

Only to hear a soft splashing noise underneath his feet.

He froze. Looked down.

Blood seeped from underneath the door. A gasp forced itself out of his throat as he took a few steps back, then looked up at Bisette's door. She was in trouble. *Is she...?*

He tried opening the door – but it stayed closed. *Locked from the inside?*

"Dr. Bisette?" He called. He heard nothing. Was she still conscious in there? "Dr. Bisette, can you hear me?!"

No response. His stomach twisted. *Could she be...?*

"What the hell is going on?" Nick turned to see Maximus approach, paling as he looked down and saw the blood. "Is that...?"

"Her door's locked," Nick blurted out, swallowing after, "and the blood is..."

"*What?*" Maximus stared down at the door, then swore, gritting his teeth. "Get out of the way, I'm picking the lock!"

Nick quickly stepped aside, letting the man get to a knee so he could pick the lock on the door. "You can pick locks?"

"Picked it up as a little skill," The other quipped as he went at the lock, "After a *few* things I went through last year. Never know when you'd need it–!"

A click echoed seconds later, and Maximus opened the door, almost falling forwards entirely. He caught himself with one hand on the ground, staining it with blood. Nick looked ahead of Maximus, realizing most of the office floor itself was stained with blood.

There was no corpse immediately seen in the room, but it was obvious there was a fight. A desk lay overturned, as well as an empty wheelchair on its side. A smashed laptop lay on the ground in pieces scattered all over the floor, with a broken cellphone against the wall on the ground, not far from it.

The most striking detail was, however, that most of the blood seeped from under the office's closet door, but enough of it trailed from it to have it pooling from the office's main doorway.

"N-no," Nick heard the man whisper. "God, *no.* Dixie…?"

Nick paused, before he sucked in a deep breath, walking towards the closet and opening it effortlessly. Was Dr. Bisette in there? Was she still alive? Maybe….

All his hopes of her still living shattered as a woman's corpse fell out of the closet, falling forwards. Despite her bloodied attire and unmoving self, it was too clear who this person was.

The killer struck again. And this time, they left behind another victim–Dr. Dixie La Bisette herself.

CHAPTER 14

Aubri immediately answered Nick's texts, after reading that there was a new victim. She, Fen, Aria, and Bastian were the first ones to make it to the crime scene, watching Nick wrap himself in his arms while another man, presumably Dr. Maximus Crispin, paced around nervously in the hall just outside the office, muttering words under his breath, trying to hold back tears.

"Nick?" Bastian ran over to Nick, wincing at the sight of Dr. Bisette's corpse before pulling Nick into a tight embrace. "Are you okay? What happened?"

"We were talking. But then she just went to her office to make a call, so I was so occupied talking with Dr. Crispin and... Someone slit her throat while she was here." Nick mumbled, keeping his head buried in Bastian's chest. "They...locked the door from the inside, so Dr. Crispin had to pick the lock, and..."

"That's..." Aubri turned to see Fen stutter, wrapping her arms around herself as she looked away, visibly shuddering. "That's the same way they found Joanna in the luggage, on that train last year!"

"Joanna?" Bastian raised a brow, looking towards Fen. "Who is she?"

Fen glanced back at him, swallowing. "One of the past victims. Former friend of mine." A sigh left her as she shook her head once. "Her corpse was stuffed into luggage and placed on a train. We thought she was expelled after bullying incidents here at the school, but…"

"Except this time," Aubri looked towards the bloody mess on the floor, and then up at Fen, "they didn't *have* time to stuff Dr. La Bisette on a train." *Hence the closet.*

Nick forced himself inhale deeply, before he looked towards Aubri, wriggling out of Bastian's arms. "Whoever did it…the murder was a sloppy job. Th-they knew they had limited time to get in and out, but Bisette probably fought them until her last breath." Nick managed. "And whoever killed her knew to lock the door on the inside, so it would be harder for anyone to go into the office. If it wasn't for Dr. Crispin picking the lock," He looked towards Crispin, who stood outside in the hallway, leaning back against the wall with his head hung, "We wouldn't get in there to see it."

"Either the criminal is really observant with doors," Aubri

heard Bastian mutter, "Or it's someone who works here. Maybe even a student."

Aubri swallowed. "S-so...it's an inside job for sure then? All these murders?"

The murderer really is part of this school?

Before anyone else could speak up, someone else did.

"Excuse me? Please move out of the way – huh?"

Nick whirled around to see a woman. She was familiar from the casino car of that engagement party train, as far as Aubri remembered. Light brown skin, dark hair and eyes, and her voice was certainly recognizable.

"Wait...Rhonda?" Nick blurted out, his head snapping towards her. "Is that you?"

Rhonda raised a brow. The neat uniform of someone attending a casino car of a train was replaced by a campus security uniform. Aubri knew that the train station lost a couple people after the whole engagement party fiasco, considering that Louise (formerly Lulu) now worked at this music school, but she hadn't realized that Rhonda herself changed jobs, too. "Wasn't expecting you here, Nick. Or any of you, honestly!"

"Neither did we." Aubri quipped. "Hi, Rhonda."

"Rhonda?" Bastian looked between her and Aubri, frowning lightly. "Wait, do you two *know* each other?"

Aubri sighed. "Remember the engagement party when your brother died? Rhonda was working in the train's casino car during then, and I interviewed her friend Ian."

"Ian told me *all* about you four after the engagement party ended." Rhonda frowned a little. "He said that if I ever ran into you again, to say hi on his behalf. He's doing fine, by the way."

"I see." Bastian looked her with an awkward grin. "Hi. Nice to meet you again, I guess."

Rhonda offered him a brief smile. "Looks like murder follows you all around, doesn't it? Now..." She looked towards Dixie's corpse, then the others, frowning, "I need all of you to tell me what you know. Immediately."

The group was quick to inform Rhonda about everything that happened, just in time for some of the other campus police to show up and start inspecting the area. Aubri was thankful they had someone on their side who wasn't just one of the police, but someone they knew well and could trust enough based on their mutual connections.

"We think it could be one of the staff, or a student." Aubri finished. "The deaths are mirroring the ones from last year to an extent...or so I think."

Before Rhonda could speak, someone else spoke up.

"What's going on?" A brown-haired woman with dark grey eyes walked towards the scene, frowning. A crisp white blouse and a pencil skirt accompanied her neat look, complete with black heels. "Officer Rhonda...?"

"There's been another murder, Dr. Reinhart. I got a call from Dr. Crispin and came as swiftly as I could." Rhonda spoke, frowning. Aubri saw her snap into a more formal response – probably expected of her duties, but it was colder in some way. "My team is inspecting the area and examining the body now."

Aubri looked towards Aria, gesturing towards Reinhart. "Who is she?" She whispered.

"Reinhart was the acting president's assistant." Aria quickly whispered back. "She was the one announcing him to have his speech, remember!?"

"Oh! Right."

Aubri looked towards Reinhart to see the woman pale at Rhonda's statement. "Who...who's the victim?"

"Dr. Bisette." Rhonda stated, keeping a straight face the

whole time. "Killed in her own office."

"Poor woman." Reinhart shook her head, before looking towards the others. "You lot found her like this?"

"Yeah." Aria cleared her throat. "I-I'm Aria, and these are my friends. Aubri, Bastian, Nick…"

"Well, nice to meet you, but…" Reinhart sighed, looking towards Aubri and the others. "I'll need all four of you to please leave this area and let the police handle the rest. We need to clean this up swiftly…."

Rhonda looked toward the group. "Thanks for the information you've already given us." She managed. "Me and my team will take it from here." With that, she stepped into the office, and Aubri overheard her speaking with the other officers already in the office about anything they might have found. Aubri wished she could go in there and see the crime scene for herself – but she probably wouldn't be allowed in.

"Surprised you're so calm about this, Dr. Reinhart." Bastian pointed out, raising a brow.

"Barely." Reinhart admitted, shaking her head. Aubri noticed her biting her lip briefly. "This is the second murder already on campus. First the acting president, and now Dr. Bisette!"

"Actually, the third one we know of." Aubri blurted out. "A student died by falling off the roof only just earlier."

Reinhart's nose wrinkled at that. "I've already cleared that up with the police. It wasn't a murder – it was a suicide."

"What?" Aria frowned. That didn't sound right! "But...the screaming at the time – I saw her body hit the ground, and it didn't look like she jumped off! And the note – I overheard the police saying it was luring her upstairs...!"

"The note was a suicide note. Her last words before her demise." Reinhart frowned, looking toward Aria. Aubri swallowed at seeing the older woman's gaze darken. "Well, if any of you learn of other *actual* murders to report, or suicide attempts, please let me or the campus police know immediately. I've already started asking students to consider staying off-campus elsewhere if they can, to minimize possible deaths, but...this is quite concerning that there's already three deaths, now."

"Did you pass by anyone leaving this building, just now?" Fen asked.

Reinhart nodded. "Well...one of the students, Lily Jiang... I think she was heading for the practice rooms, last I saw her. They're just across from this building. She has black hair in a bob, and dark brown eyes. Light olive skin. Always carries a bunny-shaped charm on her bag, too, if that helps."

"Well," Bastian managed, "Thank you, for the information." He glanced towards Aubri, starting, "Maybe we can talk to her..."

"I suggest you leave this to the police." Reinhart interrupted as she sharply looked towards him. "The last thing I need is a whole bunch of *pseudo-detectives* like what happened with last year's investigations."

Aubri noticed Fen flinch, shrinking back even as she tried speaking up. "But, Dr. Reinhart – "

"To be fair, Dr. Reinhart," Crispin spoke up, and Aubri turned to see the professor frowning, "The police were absolutely *useless* last year. I think we have good reason to keep an eye out for ourselves. And if more people want to help on the case, why not?"

"As students and relatives who *aren't* even part of this school," Reinhart countered, glaring at Aubri and the others, "You should be staying safe, not putting yourselves at risk!" She then looked toward Crispin, raising a brow. "I understand you have your qualms about last year, Dr. Crispin. But that was *last* year. If I hear about you or *these* people poking into this case any further, perhaps I'll just reconsider your continued employment."

Crispin shut his mouth, but Aubri saw him glaring at Reinhart. Reinhart ignored her, scanning the whole group with her cool gaze.

"The same goes for the rest of you, students or not. Leave this to the police. Now, if you excuse me, I must go inform Dr. Bisette's next of kin of this tragedy." Reinhart left, and Aubri did her best to ignore the click-clack of her heels as they went down the hall.

She heard Crispin sigh, and she turned to meet the other's suspicious gaze. "I don't know if I trust Reinhart." The professor huffed, crossing his arms. "I get her intentions, but she seemed awfully clammed up."

"She used to be the assistant to the previous president, right?" Aria asked. "Did anyone attempt to murder her last year?"

"No, surprisingly." Crispin shook his head, glancing toward Aubri. "The killer targeted mainly students. The only reason she targeted Dr. Bisette and Dr. Astlyr Anderson last year was because they interfered with her trying to kill other students. And speaking of students..." He frowned, glancing around, before looking toward Aubri and the others, "I should get going and check on any other students that might need help."

"Thanks for what information you could give us," Aubri managed. Crispin gave the group a nod of his head before he turned to leave.

"Based on our little chat with Reinhart, at least we know who to talk to now." Nick frowned. "And since I was with Crispin when Dr. Bisette died, we know it's not him behind it. Meanwhile, Lily is a potential suspect. And if she isn't, maybe she saw someone who approached Dr. Bisette's office while on the way out of this building."

Aria looked toward Fen. "Was Lily a student here along with you last year? Maybe we can have you introduce us to her."

"I can't. The thing is..." Fen sighed, nose wrinkling. "Lily...she doesn't exactly like me. It's going to be hard to get any of us to talk to her."

"That's not good." Aubri frowned. A lack of cooperation in any mystery never ended well. "What do we do, then?"

"What if *I* talk to Lily?" Aria spoke up. Aubri's eyes widened as she looked toward her sister – since when did Aria decide to get more proactive about solving murders like this? "I can talk to her, from student to student. She doesn't know me too well, but it's not like we've made enemies of each other yet."

"That might not be a bad idea, actually." Bastian pointed out, and Aubri noticed a grin appear on his face. "As you mentioned, Aria, you're both students. I'm sure both of you have concerns about the murders going on right now. That could be a way in to getting information from Lily."

"Are you sure about this?" Aubri looked towards Aria, placing a hand on her shoulder. "Are you going to be okay handling this yourself? Especially if she's a murder suspect..."

"Considering that I nearly got lured into being another murder victim earlier, I think I can handle talking to someone one on one. And if she does try killing me, I'll do everything to warn you." Aria swallowed, looking her in the eye. "I promise."

"Okay." Aubri just pulled her into a hug, tightly, briefly. "Just...be careful." The last thing she wanted to think of was losing another family member.

CHAPTER 15

I can't believe they have a whole building dedicated to practice rooms. That was the first thought Aria had when she entered the building on her own.

The rooms were supposed to be soundproof, but there were windows to see into the rooms on some of the doors. Aria couldn't hear the students' playing from the outside, but she could see students playing the piano or playing instruments, like the violin, or the flute, as she passed by them.

Aria soon saw Lily Jiang through one of the practice room door windows – black hair in a straight bob, hazel eyes staring at the sheet music on the music stand in front of her. She was singing. Aria noticed, in the back of the room, a bag with a bunny-shaped charm on it. The song itself was one that Aria recognized – a sung version of Mendelsohn's *On Wings of Song*. It was lovely, but there seemed to be something lacking – emotion – in her voice; at least, not the right emotion needed for a song like this one. The way she sung it almost sounded too somber for the song's overall mood.

You can do this, Aria. She coached herself, taking a deep breath. *You can talk to her. You've encountered killers before, and you've almost died, but you got through it, right? She's only a suspect – not a killer. Not that we know of, anyway.*

Why should talking to a random stranger – not that random, a student – be any different?

Aria took a deep breath and knocked on the door. Lily paused in her singing, staring towards her, before she moved towards the door, opening it.

"Sorry, but I'm going to be in here a while." Lily spoke, frowning as she eyed Aria up and down. "I know these practice rooms get filled up often, but first comes first."

"Actually, I was wondering if I can talk to you for a bit." Aria managed quickly, trying to ignore the increasing butterflies in her stomach. "You're Lily, right?"

"Yes, my name's Lily." The other student breathed, "Lily Jiang. Nice to meet you."

"We – I mean, *I* – wanted to talk to you," Aria quickly interjected, "About the murders from last year. I mean," She swallowed. Did she sound awkward? She couldn't tell.

Lily froze. Her brows furrowed, her gaze turning hard, before shaking her head lightly.

"If we're going to do this," Lily managed, "Can we at least talk in a more open space? I know this room is soundproofed, but…" She winced. "It's cramped as hell in here once you get more than one person in each room. Trust me, it's not good to have a conversation here."

Thankfully, Aria knew that this building was close enough to the main courtyard, and so she agreed to talk elsewhere. Staying in the practice room felt cramped, just as Lily said. The two went together to the courtyard in silence.

Upon entering the main courtyard, Aria found that it was empty, much to her relief, and no one would be able to hear them here, unless they walked in. She doubted anyone would be here, though – everyone was too busy hiding in their rooms or seeking off-campus shelter for their own safety right now.

She watched Lily's chest heave a bit before she spoke, looking her in the eye. "I knew someone here, who died during last year's murders." She breathed. "Her name was Siena Floros. She was heavily drugged, suffered hallucinations and…she just *died.* Right on the spot, in front of the whole class. A straight-up overdose, the police said. I knew she did drugs a little bit, but… not to the point of how much the killer put into her own food at the time."

"Almost like how the acting president died," Aria

breathed. *All the current killer's attempted murders mirroring the crimes from last year so far. Why are they deliberately doing that?*

Lily shuddered, nodding. "I wasn't a victim…I mean, no one tried to kill *me.* But when Siena died, it was like my whole world ended." She swallowed, before shaking her head. "She was one of my closest friends, and…ugh, I don't know *why* I'm rambling on about this, I'm sorry."

"No, don't be." Aria swallowed, looking towards her. "You don't have to apologize."

Lily frowned, meeting her gaze. "I admit that you're taking this pretty well. Not a lot of people want to talk about real-life murders." She paused, then asked, "Did you lose someone too?"

Aria paused. She knew that she and Lily didn't know each other that well, not really. She shouldn't really be talking about her own woes to the other. But – if they were going to be students at this school anyway, it didn't feel right for Aria to just not talk about it at some point. She knew that she'd probably end up telling someone about it at some point – so why not her?

"I…lost my father a little while ago. He got murdered, too. Not in the same way as your friend, but still. I know it can be painful."

How *did* losing a friend compare to losing someone you barely knew? Even though she barely knew her own father Leighton for long before he died, only knew about him mainly from what Bastian told her, it still felt like she lost someone.

"You lost him a while back?" Lily looked away from her, then up at her again. "How long has it been?"

Aria shrugged. "Probably six months at this point. I didn't really get to know him well before he died – it's complicated, but – part of me still kind-of misses him."

"Condolences." A sigh left Lily, before speaking up. "To be honest, I'm kind-of scared about how this is all going to go. The murders and the like. A major reason I got into this school is because my father's company regularly provides sponsorships to this school – call it nepotism, but you have to take advantage of what connections you have. My uncle, tried taking over as president after the past one died, but the position went to Dr. Dean Myers."

"Really?" That was new information. What if it was Lily's uncle who did this? "Was he...was he present, during the welcome ceremony?"

Lily shook her head quickly. "N-no. He was late. He had to use the washroom right before the ceremony started, so I sat by myself in the audience. And before you ask, he's not on campus right now – he's actually trying to get a hotel room booked for me to live in off-campus, for my safety."

Aria swallowed. "I see…"

Lily eyes flashed, and Aria flinched, seeing a deadly, sharp edge that she didn't see before. "I don't think he would murder anyone! I mean," Lily scowled, shaking her head again, "Look, I know that you and a lot of other people are concerned about who murdered who. I've heard the other students whispering about it, and I'm scared too. But I don't think my uncle did it. That's not the type of man he is, even if he is a bit competitive." She paused, then looked up at Aria. "I know this, though. Dean Myers was *nowhere* near qualified to take over as acting president."

"What? What makes you say that?" Aria frowned. "Didn't Dr. Myers graduate from this school?"

"He did, but…same with my own uncle, who graduated with *top honours*, unlike Myers." Lily's teeth grinded against each other briefly before she continued rambling on. "He's been heavily involved with helping this school's reputation, especially after the murders last year. If it wasn't for my uncle's involvement, I wouldn't still be enrolled here! For him to do all he did for this school and then they chose some *nobody* who barely got involved or kept in touch with the school, to be the acting president!?" Her hands balled into fists, "That's a load of *bullshit!*"

Aria swallowed, flinching at Lily's harsh last words, but did her best to stay calm. The way Lily's mood flipped from somber to angry, however, caught her attention – and she tried not to shudder, realizing how sudden it all was. "If it's not your uncle, though, who do you think did it?"

Lily sharply inhaled, and then she exhaled slowly. Her fists uncurled as she muttered, "Probably Astlyr. He was there when the murders happened too, you know. That guy has a scarily good memory. Wouldn't be surprised if he decided to start up a bunch of murders himself to see how well he could replicate them."

Aria wasn't convinced that made any sense. "Astylr Anderson? But what motivation would he even have?"

Lily shrugged. "The fact that he didn't become acting president this year. He didn't even make it to the interview round."

Aria tried not to frown too much. Something about all of this felt off, but she felt the need to play along with how this conversation was going. "Do you know where Astlyr might be?"

"Probably at the church." Lily shrugged. "I mean, he *is*

Head of the Pipe Organ program, after all. I'd be surprised if he wasn't there. If not, he's in his office. Should be in the building closest to the church if I'm not mistaken."

"Thank you." Aria offered her a light smile, even if she wasn't sure if it was an appropriate expression to offer, considering the subject matter. "I...appreciate you telling me all this."

"I just want the murders done and over with." Lily muttered, looking up at her, and Aria saw tears forming at the corners of her eyes. "I just want this to end, okay? Find that killer, whoever they are. I don't even know *if* it's Astlyr, but that's my best guess."

Aria stood, taking a deep breath. Astlyr Anderson...could that man be a killer?

CHAPTER 16

Aria returned to the others and explained her conversation with Lily. However, Fen was not among them as this point, since she decided to hole herself up in her room for safety.

"So, Lily said it might be Astlyr?"

Aria nodded to answer Aubri's question. "Yeah. Apparently, he tried to be president last year, but dropped out of the running even before the interview process began."

"He's part of the Pipe Organ program." Aubri noted. "I remember Fen mentioning that to me. And Louise mentioned that earlier, too."

"I see. Now that I think about it, we haven't questioned him yet." Bastian frowned lightly. "Even if he's not the killer, it wouldn't hurt to get information from him. Where is his office?"

"It's in the building closest to the church. The problem is, it's closed right now because of all the chaos with the earlier murders. Plus, today was supposed to be a day of welcoming ceremonies, so I doubt there are office hours today." Aria pointed out. "If we're going to talk to him, we'll have to wait until tomorrow."

"What do we do until then?" Bastian looked towards Nick. "Were there any other staff that you managed to talk to, other than Maximus and Dixie?"

"No." Nick shook his head. "The others were busy. And it's clear that Reinhart isn't going to let us help investigate. We should avoid talking to her, or even hinting to her that we're still investigating despite her wishes."

"Maybe we'll have better luck tomorrow." Aubri concluded. "It's getting late and think we all need some rest." She paused, looking towards Aria, and noticing her frown. "I know we already moved your things into the dorm room, but…do you want to stay over at the hotel for the night? I booked a room for the next few days. Just figured I'd offer in case you don't feel safe here."

Aria shuddered lightly. Aubri wondered if Aria was thinking about the near murder attempt she went through. "Y-yeah…I think I'll stay with you."

"That settles it, then. We're all heading off-campus for tonight." Bastian managed. "Does anyone need to use the facilities here before we find a hotel?"

"I need to use the washroom," Aria spoke up weakly, and Aubri glanced toward her. Aria didn't look so good, and Aubri's stomach twisted at seeing her so pale.

"I need to use it too." Aubri lied. "I'll go with you."

Aria offered her a light smile, nodding. The two sisters headed for the closest washroom together quickly. Aubri sighed as they entered the washroom, before speaking up. "Are you okay? You look shaken."

"Quite honestly, no." Aria swallowed, glancing toward Aubri. "It's just…when I was talking to Lily earlier, she got angry really fast."

"Like, from 0 to 100?" Aubri asked.

She watched her nod. "Yeah. That bad."

"Did she just do that randomly, or – "

Aria shook her head swiftly. "No. We were talking about the murders, and she mentioned that her uncle had also applied to get he position that Dean Myers got. She said that there was no way he could've been the murderer since he was late to the welcome ceremony."

"If that's the case," Aubri managed, "That crosses him off

our suspect list immediately."

"True. But…" Aria swallowed, recalling Lily's anger, "Something about the conversation didn't seem right. Lily, that is. I'm a bit worried. The way she freaked out didn't feel right at all. I'm not sure how to describe it further."

Aubri raised a brow. "Do you think she might be the killer, Aria? Angry on her uncle's behalf for not getting the job, so she killed Dean Myers out of vengeance?"

"I don't think we should rule it out as a possibility. A student killed last year's president, and another one could do the same." Aria nodded once, swallowing.

Aubri laid a hand on Aria's shoulder, squeezing it gently to try to comfort her.

"I'm not going to let anyone hurt you." Aubri managed. "You can count on me."

Aria offered her a smile, but it was small and weak. "I know."

CHAPTER 17

The next day, the group discussed their next steps over breakfast at the hotel, before heading back to the campus. There hadn't been any news of further murders between the time they went back to the hotel and the time they came back to campus. Classes wouldn't start for at least another week, as this week was orientation week.

However, it was too clear that the campus wasn't full of joy compared to the day before, with the welcoming festivities. Students and staff chattered quietly to each other as they made their way through the halls of the main building. Even the dorms were full of whispers of Dixie Bisette and Dean Myers' deaths, and speculation about whether there would be more.

Aubri hoped that there wouldn't be more deaths. Then again...she thought back to her time at the island resort, shuddering. That ended with a bloodbath.

Hopefully, this school wouldn't have another string of murders like last year. That was all she hoped. But three deaths were already a lot – and what if there were more?

The group figured it was best to fully join forces with Fen. Nick also called Akeno for help the other night, while they were off campus. Akeno was more than happy to offer help in any way he could. Same went with Louise, who, like Bastian and the others, didn't trust Reinhart to keep the students safe. Fen and Akeno promised to meet Aubri and the others at the dorm's entrance, so the group headed there.

Fen and Akeno both looked like they hadn't gotten much sleep. Fen especially had dark circles under her eyes, but when Aubri tried asking her about whether she needed more sleep, Fen shrugged it off and claimed she was fine.

Aubri recalled what Louise told her and the others earlier about Fen being skittish about the murders. Did the current murders keep reminding Fen too much about the other murders from last year? How many sleepless nights did she have after witnessing the murders and deaths?

How many more murders would Aubri and her friends have after they finally solved this case?

"I think I saw Dr. Anderson head to the church." Fen quipped. "We can probably find him there. Or his office."

"His office isn't far from the church." Aubri managed. "We

can search there first."

The building beside the church was relatively small. There were few offices in there, and Aubri guessed this must be the equivalent of a church office, if anything. There was a small, main reception area, and after inquiring about Astlyr Anderson, the group was allowed to enter Astlyr's office and speak to him privately.

"Please, have a seat." Astlyr Anderson opened the office door to let them in. His blond hair, tied back in a short ponytail, was pale and showed greying strands. The lines on his forehead made him look weary. Tired. Aubri could tell by his eyes, despite the slight smile he had. The smile faded, however, as he spoke. "I heard that you wanted to speak to me. Is there something the matter?"

Aubri swallowed as she and the others moved to sit down. She waited for Astlyr to sit down before speaking. There was no really good way to say it, so she just blurted it out. "It's about the murders on campus."

His eyes darkened immediately at Aubri's statement. A sigh left him before he asked, "You must be more specific. Is it the ones from yesterday, last year, or about twenty years ago?"

Aubri noticed Nick shudder at the last part of that

statement, from the corner of her eye, but she shook her head. "The ones from yesterday, I meant. I'm sorry if it brings up any... bad memories."

"I guess I can't not talk about it." A sigh left him after. "Go ahead, shoot. What do you want to know?"

"You're fine with us asking you?" Aubri raised a brow. "Just like that?" If there was anything she learned from reading and watching all the fictional murder mysteries, sometimes those too willing to help with solving crimes were often the criminals themselves – make themselves look trustworthy so no one would think they were the culprit. Nessandra nearly did the same thing back on the train, during the engagement party of the then-murdered Leighton Faulkner. What if Astlyr was the same?

"I've heard Reinhart tell the whole lot of us staff to not help anyone that wasn't police, but...I don't trust the police to accomplish finding the killer successfully, let alone do *anything* to protect our students." A snarl left him at that. "Despite the whole fiasco from last year, the board still didn't bother expanding the budget for security! How many more deaths is it going to take?"

Aubri noticed Bastian frown. "Sounds like you're rather dissatisfied with how things are going. Honestly, I don't blame you given everything."

"Of course, I'm unhappy about it!" Astlyr frowned, looking up at Bastian and the others as he kept speaking. "Dr. Dean Myers walked into this school all new. Just because he graduated from this place doesn't mean he's kept in touch with its inner workings. Hell," A low chuckle left him, shaking his head once, "I don't even remember him being a very good student at the school. He and I were classmates and graduated in the same year."

"And you think you'd do a better job than him?" Bastian immediately asked afterward.

Astlyr raised a brow. "I never said anything about me being any better than him, did I?"

"Dr. Anderson..." Nick started, but Astlyr shook his head.

"Look, I *get* it. I can see why you're all hounding me. You heard that I tried to become the acting president, didn't you?" Astlyr leaned back in his chair, staring up at Aubri. The corner of his lips turned to a frown, ever so slightly. "I *am* kind-of pissed that I didn't get the job. But at the same time..." A sigh left him, and he shook his head. "I've made my peace with it. I'm not sure what I was thinking, trying to become the next president – I honestly applied on a whim. I *like* working at this place, and

I do enjoy the opportunities I get to keep the art of practicing pipe organ alive, by being Head of this program. And considering what happened last year...would I *want* to be in a position of covering up things?" He visibly shuddered.

"Yeah, I can see why you wouldn't want to take on being the president after what really happened last year." Aubri frowned.

Astlyr nodded, glancing toward her. Now that she got a better look at his face, Aubri realized that he wasn't just tired – he was completely burnt out. "I don't think I want to be the one handling the entire aftermath myself. Especially with these new murders happening."

"Do you have any idea who might've done it? This year, that is?"

"I don't know." Astlyr swallowed, and Aubri noticed a certain distant look appear in his eyes. His gaze softened as he looked towards Aubri. "I honestly don't know. But if you do find out who it is, you better stop them before they cause a complete massacre out of this place – one so bad that this school will never recover from."

The group left Astlyr be – they needed time to

think through everything and everyone they'd talked to and witnessed. And after seeing how tired Astlyr was during their conversation, it made Aubri wonder if there were other staff just tired and burnt out. It would explain why there wasn't as much staff to begin with during this term, for sure.

"I don't think the killer is Astlyr." Aria stretched her arms behind her as she spoke, looking between Bastian, Nick, and Aubri. "He doesn't have a motive for killing Dr. Myers. That's pretty obvious – especially if he's already at peace with not becoming the president to begin with."

"Was he telling the truth, though?" Bastian frowned, shaking his head. "He did seem pretty pissed to not get the acting president role. And you know how serious he got about the lack of security on campus."

Nick nodded, looking towards Bastian. "I agree with Aria. Body language gave it away – you could tell he was certainly anxious about all the deaths. If anything, it shows how passionate he is about this school."

'Or he's a *great* actor." Aubri interjected, frowning.

Bastian sighed, scratching the back of his head briefly. "Well, he seems the least likely to be the killer. Besides, Fen is one of his own students, and even she was already freaked out from last year's murders. Do you honestly think that he'd want to further traumatize and/or potentially kill his own students?"

"You have a point." Nick glanced between Bastian and Aubri. "It's probably not him, considering that fact. But then, who else can we ask or suspect, even?"

"Maybe Louise would know more information." Aria pointed out. "Surely, she knows of who else might've tried to be acting president, right? It can't just be Lily's uncle and Astlyr. There could be more candidates we don't even know of, yet."

"We should chat with her, then." Bastian managed. "She's probably back in her office, where we last saw her. If not, maybe we can ask the other staff and see if there's anyone else with ill will toward Myers?

"Yeah, that sounds like a good plan. Should we split up?" Aubri asked. "That way, we can cover more ground faster. Besides, we might look super-suspicious if we stick together, especially if we run into Reinhart. Aria can go with me and pretend she's giving me a tour, and...uh..." She faltered, scanning the others. "Do you guys want to pair up or something?"

Fen looked towards Nick. "Maybe I can go with you?"

Nick nodded in agreement, before looking towards

Bastian. "Bastian…?"

"I can stick with Akeno." Bastian reassured him. "Let's get going, okay?"

Aubri noticed Nick smile lightly back at him. "Okay."

CHAPTER 18

The group soon split up, and Bastian and Akeno went on their way to Louise's office. The other two groups headed elsewhere on campus, hoping to speak with some other staff or students about the previous murders.

It didn't take long for Bastian to find Louise's office, knocking.

No answer. He tried opening the door, only to realize it was locked.

"Bastian," Akeno started, "She's out."

It was only then that he noticed the "Be back soon" sign on the door. A sigh left Bastian as he looked toward Akeno. "Oh. Guess we'll have to find her elsewhere, then."

He felt the phone in his pocket vibrate, and he took it out to see a text from Louise:

Found these files. Thought they might be helpful for finding the killer in case it's one of the students. Dr. Reinhart announced to all the students that they're supposed to leave campus starting today for their safety. She already scheduled leave times for each of them, too. If one of them is the killer, you have limited time left.

"Bastian?" Akeno asked. "Is something wrong?"

Before anyone else could speak up, a shot echoed from outside. Bastian jumped as looked around, trying to find its source. Was it the killer striking *again?* Why do this during the day?   That shot didn't sound far from the main courtyard, either - or at least that was where Bastian heard it from. He instinctively started walking faster, before breaking into a run. What if it was an innocent student in danger? Or one of the other staff?

Despite the questions swirling in his mind, nothing could prepare him to see none other than Louise Anders lying on the ground in the middle of the courtyard, gasping for breath. Her hands laid over her own abdomen, blood seeping past her fingers and dripping onto the cement ground underneath her, cellphone broken and on the ground beside her.

"Louise!" Bastian wasted no time getting to a knee by Louise's side, taking off his coat and putting it over her abdomen. He tried putting pressure on it as he looked towards her paling face. "Louise? Stay with me! What *happened?*"

"I…just got out of my office a-and texted you…" Louise coughed, and Bastian tried not to grimace at seeing the blood from her lips. "They…shot…"

"I heard the gunshot. Do you remember what they looked like?" He struggled to keep a hand over her abdomen to apply pressure, while taking his phone out of his pants pocket, and he was grateful he had the police on speed dial at this point. "I need you to stay with me, okay?"

Louise nodded, swallowing, but then she coughed again. Bastian heard the tone ring as he held the cellphone to his ear before a voice spoke up.

"9-1-1–"

"There's an emergency. My friend has been shot." Bastian wasn't sure how he managed to keep his voice from mostly cracking, but he did. "I'm with her right now, I put pressure on her wound, but she's been bleeding out pretty fast since I got here."

"Can you tell me where you and your friend are?"

"At the music school. Main courtyard. Please come quickly!"

There was a pause, and then the other spoke up. *"We've sent an ambulance. They'll be coming in ten to fifteen minutes. Keep that pressure on your friend's wound, okay? Don't move her from where she is."*

"Okay." Bastian swallowed, looking down at Louise, at his hands and his jacket keeping pressure on her wound, stained with her blood. He heard her breathe through her mouth, and all he could do, in that moment, was pray and hope that she made it through. That the ambulance would be here soon.

That she'd live.

CHAPTER 19

Bastian and Akeno accompanied Louise all the way to the campus' medical centre, but he was forced to stay in the waiting room after the staff took her in for emergency surgery and treatment. He paced back in forth in the drab waiting room. The walls were cream-white but tinted with grey undertones, and he closed his eyes, hoping that the lack of this hospital scene might help him focus and force his worries away.

"Bastian?"

He opened his eyes to see Aubri rush over to him, followed closely by Aria, Fen...

And Nick.

Bastian went straight to Nick, and his lover pulled him into his arms tightly. Bastian buried his head into Nick's shoulder, forcing himself to take a deep breath.

"I heard you came here." Nick rasped, and Bastian pulled his head away briefly to see pure worry in his lover's eyes. "Are you okay? What happened?"

Bastian let it all spill out; hearing the gunshot, running into the courtyard to find Louise bleeding out alone. Calling for help, begging her to stay with him, to stay alive—and then he couldn't make himself speak anymore.

She could have *died* today, he realized. She could have died, all because she helped them with the case. How the killer knew that fact, he didn't know, but…how many more did the killer plan on murdering to silence anyone and everyone possible?

"Probably the killer." Bastian heard Akeno mutter. "There's no one else I could think of doing it. Is she okay?"

"She'll be fine, I think." Bastian swallowed. Despite what he said, he couldn't help but ask himself, *would* she? She almost died.

And it was his fault.

Aubri noticed how pale and shaky Bastian was. The last time she saw him this mortified, it was back during the engagement party fiasco. Maybe it was best to see how he was without being surrounded by all their friends. "Bastian? Can we talk privately for a sec?"

Bastian wordlessly nodded. He followed her a little

further down the main hall before Aubri spoke up. "Are you okay?"

"Fuck no, I'm not." He shook his head, and Aubri thought she saw a few tears gathering at the corners of his eyes – real, horrified tears, nothing like the crocodile tears she remembered Renee giving her back at the Calloway Resort. "She almost *died*, Aubri!"

"And you saved her." Aubri interjected.

His gaze snapped towards her, and she realized how reddened his eyes were. "*Only* because I was close enough to the main courtyard from where I called her! If I was on the other side of campus and no one else reached her…if I didn't, she'd be dead right now."

"Please, calm down."

"I am not calming down!" Bastian sat down in the closest chair, running his hands through his own hair as he forced himself to breathe, then pushed it all out in a single breath. Another inhale and exhale later, he sighed, swallowing as he looked up at her. "I'm sorry, okay? I just…"

"I know it's a lot." Aubri swallowed, sitting down beside him, trying to make eye contact. "And I'm sorry. I just…you shouldn't blame yourself for her getting hurt. It's the killer's fault."

"It's hard not to." He shook his head. "We pulled her into this case, Aubri. Or rather, *I* did."

"She could have easily refused to help us." Aubri pointed out, frowning. "But she *chose* to help us. It's not the first time she helped us, either. She knew the risks."

"It was different, back during the engagement party when my brother got killed. She was a suspect, not a potential victim. But now..." He looked towards the room where Louise was, and then towards Aubri, shaking his head, "Now she almost died. And more and more innocent people like her *will* get targeted, solely because they're trying to help us find out who murdered the president."

"It's not too late to stop whoever's committing these murders." Aubri took Bastian's hand in hers, squeezing it. "We'll figure this out. We've done this twice before, and we can do it again. Don't lose hope, okay?"

Bastian swallowed once, nodding. He was about to speak again when Aria's voice echoed down the hallway.

"Um, Aubri? Bastian?" The two turned to see Aria calling to them, and she swallowed, approaching them. "Are you two okay?"

"We're better now." Bastian managed, looking towards her, and Aubri thought that Bastian might be smiling lightly, even if briefly. "What is it?"

"Er...the killer's identity." Aria fidgeted a bit, gazed down at her hands folded together and then up at the other two. "I think I know who it is."

"What?" Both Aubri and Bastian exchanged shocked looks before they raced over to rejoin Aria and the others.

Fen frowned lightly, looking towards her. "Who do you think it is?"

Aria swallowed, then stated, "Lily Jiang. It can't be anyone else but her."

CHAPTER 20

"What do you *mean,* you think it was Lily!?" Fen burst out, staring at Aria. "She was present during the welcome ceremony!"

"As an alibi." Aria managed, looking towards her. "She's one of the richest students in this entire school. Her father's company is a regular sponsor. On top of that, her uncle *tried* to become acting president, but was denied the opportunity despite having more qualifications than Dean Myers…or so Lily claimed, at least, when I spoke with her."

Aria swallowed, trying to gauge the other's expressions. Bastian looked a bit stunned, Fen visibly paled, and Aubri was quiet, brows furrowing but saying nothing. Aria kept talking, trying to explain further. "She was angry when she was mentioning that to me, too. Besides, she also would have decent-enough knowledge of the murders. She witnessed one of her best friends, Siena Floros, dying in a way like Dr. Myers did in the past. She heard about the other ones happening on campus last year too!"

"But even if she had experience or at least ideas for murdering people based off last year's murders," Nick asked, frowning, "and a potential motivation with jealousy as you mentioned...*how* would she know how to murder Dr. Myers the way he died? And why bother targeting the other students and staff, if he was the main victim in mind?"

"She's been a student for at least two years, too, so she'd know the campus inside-out." Aria answered. At least, it made sense to her that Lily would know the main routes on campus if she was here the year before. "And she probably targeted the other students and staff out of vengeance over her best friend dying and the killer being found way too late at the time. Her uncle not becoming the president probably helped fuel the anger she already had. She tried killing the other students and staff to silence and scare them by repeating the same types of murders from last year before they could make the connection to her being a copycat."

"Aria might have a point." Akeno managed, frowning. Despite the situation they were talking about, Aria felt gratitude sink in – especially with the acknowledgement coming from none other than a fellow student. "And all the victims, save for Louise, were people involved in the murders from last year – both those investigating, *and* those who nearly died."

"So that made the attempt on Louise's life collateral damage, then?" Nick asked, and Aria watched Bastian visibly wince at the way his boyfriend worded it. "Because she was helping us put those connections together?"

"Exactly. And Lily probably picked up on us investigating the murders because I talked to her, to begin with!" Aria concluded. She shuddered at thinking of anyone as 'collateral damage,' but if she were the killer…she'd want to get rid of anyone in the way of their plans, right? "We have to find Lily and stop her from killing anyone else, and fast!"

"I saw Lily heading to her dorm building an hour ago." Akeno noted, frowning. "She looked like she was in a rush."

"She could be trying to escape." Bastian managed quickly, frowning. "Before Louise was shot, she sent me a text telling me that the staff encouraged the students to find shelter elsewhere off-campus. Lily might be using that opportunity as a cover."

"Yes." Akeno nodded quickly. "As TA, I can confirm that the students each have scheduled leave times to ensure they got off campus safely. Staff was supposed to leave after all students evacuated, too."

Bastian swallowed, glancing down at his cellphone, and Aria noticed him speak up. "And…based on what Louise sent me,

Lily's scheduled to leave *today,* according to Louise's files that she sent us. In one hour from now."

"What!?" A gasp left Aubri, eyes widening. "We have to get to her and stop her from leaving campus!"

"I'll call the campus police immediately and let them know the situation." Akeno quipped, taking out his cellphone. "You guys go to the dorms ahead of me!"

"Okay!"

"Aria?" Aubri looked towards her sister. "You know this campus a little better than I do–which way is it to the dorm again?"

Aria knew she had no choice but to take the lead on this one, or else everyone else would get lost. "This way! Quickly!"

CHAPTER 21

The group ran straight to the dorm building – they weren't far from the campus medical centre, so it didn't take long to get there at all. Aria was the first to head in through the front doors, noticing the person at the front desk as she spoke up.

"Excuse me, but have you seen Lily Jiang enter this building recently?"

The person at the front desk shrugged. "Oh, Lily? She went to her room not long ago. She hasn't left yet."

"Which floor?" Bastian asked.

The front desk person raised a brow. "Is there something wrong?"

"She *murdered* a whole bunch of students and staff." Akeno snapped, glaring at them. "The police are on their way right now and we have to make sure she doesn't escape!"

An audible gasp left the other, before she stuttered, "M-murder!? Er, she's on the…the th-third floor. She's the only one up there. Room 310!"

"That's my floor!" Aria gasped. "I'm room 303!"

"Thank you." Nick spoke to the attendant, who simply nodded, too frightened to say anything else. With that, the whole group ran to the stairs. Aubri knew that running for the elevator was useless; it was likely the route Lily would take to get downstairs to prevent herself from being intercepted and waiting for an elevator to go upstairs was too long. The stairs would just have to do.

Aria was the first to make it to the top of the stairs and head onto the third floor, running straight to Lily's room. As she caught her breath, standing in front of the door, she knew that it was now or never – she had to stop a murderer from killing her fellow students and staff.

Even if it meant betraying one of the few students she knew best out of everyone here.

Aria took a deep breath and knocked on the door. "Lily?"

No answer. Aria frowned. That didn't seem right. Usually, Lily was quick to answer. She knocked again. "Lily? Open up, please! I know what you did!"

No answer again.

She heard Bastian curse, and she turned to realize that he and the others caught up with her. "Is anyone good at picking locks, here?"

Aria heard someone clear their throat, and she turned to see Akeno catch up, panting for breath. "Allow me! I've got security on the way just now and I ran as fast as I could to catch up…"

Everyone stepped aside so Akeno could pick the lock. Immediately after an audible click was heard, he pushed the door open –

Just in time to see the corpse of Lily Jiang, hanging on a rope tied to the ceiling fan. Aria also noticed a tipped-over chair underneath her body.

Aria gagged and looked away instinctually. She heard Aubri gasp as Akeno swore, and Fen's scream rang over everyone.

Aria, despite her utter revulsion for finding dead bodies at this point, forced herself to look towards the corpse that was once her classmate.

"L-Lily?"

It had to be some kind of sick joke, right? *Lily would never…would she?*

As the others reacted to the corpse, Aubri forced herself to look around and tried not eyeing the corpse too much. It was obvious how Lily died, but why take her own life like this? Did she realize she was caught? Was she feeling guilty about what she did so soon?

Something didn't make sense, here. As she looked around, she noticed that there was a folded-up piece of paper on the desk, and she opened it up, reading:

For those that find this, please take this as my personal admission of murdering Dr. Myers, Dr. La Bisette, and another student as well as attempting to murder m Ms. Anders. I sincerely regret all the harm I've caused to this year's staff and students alike, and I believe that going out this way was the best I could do.

There was no signature.

"A suicide?" Nick whispered.

Aubri looked up to see Bastian swallowing at the sight. "I think it was."

"An actual suicide note?" Fen walked over to Aubri. "Can I take a look?"

"Yeah." Aubri showed it to her. She watched Fen's brows furrow as she read it, only to shake her head.

"This wasn't a suicide." She spoke, looking up at her from the note. "This was a murder."

Aubri frowned. "How can it be a murder? The note's there. No one else came up to her room!"

"Lily was alone when she died." Fen pointed out. "Or so the front desk person thought. But...this note isn't in her own handwriting. *Someone* had to be up there with her just now."

"Are there any ways to get downstairs, other than the stairs we took going up?"

Aria swallowed. "This building has stairs as part of safety standards and all, but...we also have an elevator here. The killer's in the elevator then, right? On the way down?"

"Maybe..."

A loud bang came from downstairs, and everyone froze.

"Was that...?" Bastian breathed, but Nick swallowed.

"I'll go check." Nick was about to head out the door when Aubri noticed Bastian grab his wrist, stopping him.

"Nick? Be careful." Bastian sounded hoarse, and Aubri didn't blame him for sounding so worried. After all, Louise almost died not long ago, and Bastian blamed himself for that already. If his boyfriend died, then...

Nick gave Bastian a brief kiss on the cheek. "I will." He whispered back, before giving him another kiss. Aubri tried to force herself to relax – she knew that Nick wasn't about to let himself die that easily. Not today. But as she watched him go, after Akeno insisted on coming downstairs with him, she just hoped that both would be okay.

In the meantime – she, Bastian, Fen, and Aria had to try to find more clues.

Nick and Akeno both made it downstairs as fast as they could, taking the stairs. The elevator would've taken too much time to pursue the murderer – at least, that was what Nick guessed from all the shows he and Bastian saw together. As they did so, they walked into the main reception area…

Only to find the receptionist at the desk, slumped over in her chair as she bled out from her chest. Akeno rushed over to her as a gasp tore from his throat. He leaned over the desk and put a hand to her neck to check for a pulse. Nick noticed Akeno shake his head, withdrawing his hand.

"She's gone." Akeno muttered as his eyes met Nick's own. "The murderer must've killed her to get rid of possible witnesses."

"*Freeze!*"

Both men whirled around to see Rhonda and a few other

security officers run into the building, two of them raising guns.

Nick held both his hands up, and he noticed Akeno do the same as he spoke up. "We found her dead just now! And one of the other students is dead upstairs, on the third floor! Our friends are still up there when we found them together!"

"What?" Rhonda motioned for some of the officers to run ahead to the stairs, before she approached Nick, Akeno, and the corpse, frowning. "What happened?"

"The killer was just here." Akeno managed, swallowing. "Whoever it was, they...they killed Lily and planted a false suicide note. The receptionist was still alive before we found Lily's corpse upstairs...so the killer was on their way out when they killed her."

"That means they just left the building before we arrived!" Rhonda's eyes widened, before taking out her walkie-talkie, speaking into it. "I need Unit 3 to scope the west side of campus immediately! The killer just left the student dorms!"

As Rhonda was preoccupied with giving orders, Aubri and the others came downstairs to the main floor a few minutes later. Nick heard Aria audibly gasp at seeing the dead receptionist, just as Bastian raced over to Nick.

"What happened?"

Nick swallowed as he looked toward Bastian. "The receptionist got killed on the way out. Killer probably wanted to silence any potential witnesses. A-Akeno and I were too late to help, and Rhonda and security came in just after we did."

"That explains why we had three security guards questioning us about what happened a minute ago." Bastian muttered. He wrapped an arm around Nick, just as Aubri spoke up.

"Akeno? I have a question. Does the hanging resemble any of the murders from last year?"

Akeno gritted his teeth but nodded. "It does. Lionel Bayrak, a second-year student, was murdered last year. The killer planted a false suicide note, but we didn't realize it was false until much later…"

"What *type* of murder will the killer try next?"

He stared at her. "Why are you asking this now?"

"The current murderer is copying every single attempted murder from *last year.*" Aubri pointed out. "So far, we've had a student pushed off the roof to their death and it being framed as a suicide, Louise being shot, Dr. Myers drugged with deadly dosages, and Dr. Bisette was stabbed and left to bleed out in a hidden area – the closet of her own office. Now Lily was hanged with a false suicide note too, with the killer trying to frame her for the previous murders on top of that. I think any other remaining types of murders could determine where the killer will strike next, since we confirmed earlier that they're a copycat. Are there any other murders that happened last year that haven't happened in the present yet?"

Akeno faltered, then a gasp left him. "Drowning." He rasped. "Meghan Ishikawa's near-murder by drowning! The killer's taking their next victim to the campus' swimming pool to recreate that murder. That's where Meghan almost died…"

"Then we need to head to the pool, and fast." Nick cut in. "They probably have a victim in mind already. And with the security buckling down on campus, they probably want to finish this string of murders *right now.*"

CHAPTER 22

The entire group ran for the campus pool, and Akeno was quick to call campus police and ask them to send officers to the campus pool in case. As they entered the campus' athletics center, Aubri winced as she noticed that there was a person at the front desk already dead, their brains blown out behind them as the corpse slumped back in their chair.

"The killer's already here." She managed, swallowing. "Which way is the pool?"

"Follow me!" Akeno took the lead, and the others quickly followed. They made it down the main hall, turning a sharp left, and through the locker rooms. As they made it into the main pool area, they found the following sight:

Maximus Crispin was bound and gagged, hands tied behind his back, forced to stand at the deep end of the main pool. The other person standing beside him quickly put a gun to his head. Her spare hand kept a firm grip on one of his arms.

"Don't move." The killer spoke. Aubri recognized the dark brown hair, tied back in a neat bun, as well as the steely, gray eyes they had.

"Dr. Reinhart?" She heard Nick gasp. "What the hell are you doing!?"

Dr. Stella Reinhart glared towards the group, keeping the gun against Maximus' head. "You heard me—don't move! If you do, this one's getting their brains blown out. Or I shove him into the pool, and he drowns."

"I know which method you planned on using." Aubri managed, meeting Reinhart's gaze. "You're copying last year's murders. Why?"

Reinhart's nostrils flared as she returned the look. "I was supposed to be the next acting president. Everyone knew that I'd worked at this school for *years.* When I found out they were seeking a new president, I tried to get an interview. I would've gotten it, but..."

"Myers got the job." Aubri pieced together.

"Dr. Myers was the least qualified out of all the final candidates! There's no way he should've gotten the role unless he bribed or blackmailed HR himself!" She snapped, hands shaking despite keeping the gun close to Crispin's head. "*I* should've been the new acting president, after all I've done for this school! When all those staff members and students ran away with their tails between their legs, who stayed? Me! I was *loyal.* I was born for greater things than being some *assistant* to the president."

"Well, you're certainly going down in history as a *serial killer.*" Bastian quipped, raising a brow. "The police are already on their way here! Trying to add more victims to your already-long list isn't going to help you. If you surrender and cooperate with them and us, maybe you'll get a lighter sentence. Maybe."

"I've gone too far to go back. And once I'm done with him and the whole lot of you, no one will ever realize it's me and I'll finally get what I *deserve!*" That was when she pointed the gun at the group and fired.

A shot rang out, and Nick heard Akeno gasp, stumbling backwards before falling to the ground. Blood started staining his shirt, from his left shoulder, and Nick's eyes widened as he rushed to Akeno's side. "Akeno!"

Reinhart pushed the still struggling and bound Maximus into the pool with her spare hand, a loud splash accompanying the man as he sank underneath the waters instantly.

"Shit!" Bastian took off his coat. "I'm going in after him!" He didn't hesitate to dive into the pool, likely heading after

Maximus. Aubri quickly followed, not even bothering to take off her shoes or coat as she dove into the pool.

"You are not!" Reinhart pointed her gun at Bastian, pulling the trigger, but no bullet sounded. A hiss left her as she pulled the trigger again, but nothing happened. "Dammit!"

"I-I'm fine," Akeno rasped, as Nick grabbed Akeno's hands and forced them to keep pressure on his wound. "G-go after her!"

"No!" Nick still struggled to keep pressure on the wound with his own hands on top of Akeno's own. Despite his best efforts, blood was getting on his and Akeno's hands already. "I'm not losing you!"

Aria looked between Reinhart, and Akeno and Nick, before looking towards Reinhart again. Reinhart's gun wasn't working, right? Maybe this was her chance to at least stop her before she could escape and kill someone else.

"You bitch!" Aria didn't care how she sounded as she ran at Reinhart. She knew she couldn't stand back in fear. She wasn't going to let anyone else die tonight if she could do something about that!

Reinhart tried backing up a few feet, pointing her gun at Aria rushing towards her. She pulled the trigger, but no bullet emerged. Aria neared her, and tackled her down to the pool floor, pinning her down as best as she could.

Both women groaned as they hit the pool deck. Aria tried to spread her whole body flat against Reinhart to keep her pinned down. Reinhart wasn't going down without a fight, however, trying to push and shove Aria off her.

"Let go," Reinhart rasped, "Or else…"

"No!" Aria flinched as Reinhart struck her in the face. Despite that, she punched the older woman even harder in the face in response, trying to keep her down. She hit her again, backhanding her this time, and she heard Reinhart gasp for breath.

She couldn't remember exactly how the rest of their struggle went – it was a flurry of limbs, both women trying to push and shove each other out of the way.

That was when Aria noticed a glint of metal from the corner of her eye as Reinhart took out something from her inner jacket pocket – another gun? Was it loaded?

Aria noticed Bastian surface with Maximus and Aubri from the corner of her eye. The three desperately reached the shallow end of the pool, trying to climb out quickly. Reinhart pointed the gun at them, aiming. Without thinking, Aria lunged forwards, slapping the hand that held the gun hard. The gun flew out of Reinhart's hands, sliding across the pool deck.

"You..!" Reinhart tried punching Aria in the face, but Aria ducked out of the way, trying to kick her in the leg. She took a quick peek around her, the sight of Nick struggling to keep pressure on Akeno's wound and Bastian and Aubri now pulling Maximus out of the water greeting her.

That was a mistake.

A sharp force knocked against the Aria's side, from Reinhart pushing her hard, elbow digging into her ribs. Aria stumbled, but she rebalanced herself quickly before she could completely fall over. As she regained her balance, she turned to see Reinhart pointing the gun it at her.

"Don't move." Reinhart hissed. Before she could do anything, Aria heard a gasp from the right. she looked towards the right to see Nick pointing the other gun at Reinhart.

"A-actually," Nick spoke up, trying to keep his voice as calm as possible while pointing the other gun at Reinhart, "It's you that shouldn't be moving."

He couldn't believe that he was doing this. He never expected to one day pick up a gun and threaten someone, but here he was now – and now he had a serial killer to stop from killing his own friends. Akeno was bleeding out a few feet behind him, Aria and Reinhart were right in front of him, and the others were too preoccupied with saving Dr. Crispin – and who knows how soon the police would arrive?

Reinhart's eyes widened, before pointing her gun at Nick, but he knew it would be fruitless. *"What?"*

"Don't pull that trigger!" His voice came out as a snarl. "Or *else...*"

"Or else *what?*" A brief laugh left Reinhart as she shook her head. "That gun you're holding is empty, you fool!"

Nick raised a brow. "Is it?"

Nick heard Bastian gasp behind him. "Nick, watch out...!"

Reinhart pointed her gun at him, pulling the trigger. Nick's stomach twisted – only for it to relax as he realized *nothing* happened. No bullet, just - *nothing.*

It was oddly satisfying to see Reinhart gasp. Any excitement Nick had about it shortly died when she glared at him. "You switched my guns!?"

"While you and Aria were both on the ground, yeah." Nick kept his gun pointed at her. It was a cool trick he'd seen in those murder mystery shows, the ones he and Bastian binge-watched together. Despite all the actual murders he'd been around in his life, for once he was grateful that he could use something from fiction to handle a very real situation right now. "Get away from Aria and drop your gun, *now.*"

Reinhart glared at Aria and Nick. She then took a deep breath, dropping her gun – only to run at Aria, trying to push her into the pool. Nick pulled the trigger –

A bang echoed through the room.

Reinhart staggered mid-motion, a weak gasp leaving her lungs, before falling into the pool. Aria stumbled out of the way of Reinhart's body falling into the water. Nick could only watch as Aria's eyes widened, looking away as blood from Reinhart's head started staining the water.

It only then registered to Nick what he'd done.

"O-oh *god.*" Nick dropped the gun, hands shaking. His knees gave away, and he felt the harsh ground against his knees. He forced himself to take a deep breath and closed his eyes, trying not to imagine Reinhart bleeding out in the pool in front of him. "Wh-what did I…?"

Why? He didn't have to shoot – but he did – *why?*

"Nick?" It was Bastian calling – Nick felt his hand on his shoulder, heard the other whispering to him worriedly. "Are you okay?"

"N-no." Nick felt his face warm a bit – not from embarrassment but from tears forming in the corners of his eyes. "Just…stay. Please."

"I'm right here." He felt Bastian squeeze his shoulder, and there was some relief in his touch. "I'm right here and I'm not leaving you, okay? The police are on their way."

"I killed her –"

"I know," Bastian stressed, "and you were trying to protect Aria and the rest of us."

"I-I didn't mean to –"

"I know you didn't. I know you didn't, okay?" Nick tried to rub the tears away with the back of his hand, looking up at Bastian. The older man's eyes widened at seeing him, before pulling him into a tight hug. "I'm right here."

From the corner of his eye, he noticed a soaking-wet Maximus Crispin rushing to Akeno, police rushing into the pool area as Aubri and Aria hurriedly explained the situation.

"It's over." Bastian whispered to Nick. "It's over. We're safe now, it's *okay.*"

Nick wasn't sure if it really was okay.

CHAPTER 23

The police soon arrived at the pool. Aubri and the others explained what happened, and Akeno and Maximus Crispin were both rushed to the campus' medical centre to be looked after. Thankfully, Akeno would survive since the bullet missed his vital organs. The wound wasn't s bad as it looked, and he was less seriously hurt than anticipated. Maximus also lived, thanks to Aubri and Bastian saving him from drowning. Nick wouldn't be charged for murdering Reinhart, for his act of self-defence.

Fen was in Akeno's hospital room, visiting him. Bastian and Aria both went to get some snacks and drinks from the vending machines, hoping that food would calm everyone's nerves. Nick, meanwhile, paced around in the waiting room, and Aubri sat in one of the chairs, watching him. She knew that he already visited Akeno and knew that he would be fine. However, Nick was still clearly in shock from Reinhart's death. A sigh left her as she pushed a few bangs out of her face.

"Nick? You want to sit down?" Aubri started. "You look like you're going to collapse if you don't get some rest. I know..." She swallowed. "I know it must be hard on you."

A sigh left Nick as he approached her, sitting down on a chair beside her. He sunk into his seat, and he looked up at her after a moment.

"I *killed* someone tonight." His voice sounded incredibly hoarse. Aubri thought his eyes might be red. However, she wasn't sure if he cried sometime between Reinhart's death and now, or if it was a trick of the light. "I-I murdered someone, Aubri...she was *alive,* and...I thought...she was going to kill Aria if I didn't do anything." He bent forward, buried his head in his hands briefly, running his hands through his hair. He shook his head as he looked up at her again. "I was only trying to disarm her or at least distract her, not *kill* her. I couldn't lose Aria and Akeno to Reinhart, Aubri."

"You were trying to defend Aria and the others." Aubri told him, struggling to make eye contact with him. "It was only self-defence."

"I-I'm not a murderer, Aubri...I don't want to *be* a murderer."

"You're *not.*" A sigh left her, before she finally made eye contact with him. "Look, I get it. I've been there. I know it sucks that you pulled the trigger because of everything that happened – because you feel like you didn't know what else to do. I felt similarly when I let go of Renee and she fell to her death."

"Wait, what?" He stared at her, eyes widening. He just stared up at her, stunned, before asking, "She didn't just…tip over the balcony railing?"

"She kind-of did, but I caught her by the wrist at the last minute. I even considered pulling her to safety, despite her trying to murder me and Bastian at the time." Aubri admitted, swallowing. She tried her best not to visualize the entire situation as she kept talking, but she knew that it would keep haunting her for a while still. Even now, she occasionally heard her ex-girlfriend's pleas for safety in the back of her mind. "But then she tried to stab me…and I let go of her."

"Sorry." Nick ducked his head briefly, before looking up at her again, visibly swallowing. "I just…I can't imagine how that felt for you."

"I still carry a bit of guilt." She admitted. "And to be honest, I don't know if it'll fade away. But…don't let this drag you down. You didn't mean to straight-up kill them." She reached a hand towards his shoulder, placing it there, hoping to reassure him as his gaze met hers. "You're not some remorseless serial killer, Nick. If you were, you wouldn't be fretting over killing them in the first place."

"But…" Nick started, but Aubri frowned.

"I'm not done talking – and besides, you saved Aria too! I don't know what would've happened if you didn't intervene with Reinhart fighting her. And in a way, you saved potential future victims from dying." After all, a serial killer couldn't kill people if she was already dead. "You saved a lot more people than you think, Nick."

"I don't know." He admitted, with another shake of his head. "I don't feel like I saved anyone."

"You did." She insisted. "I know this pain isn't going to get any easier to deal with. Just remember you tried to do the right thing, okay?"

"Yeah..." Nick trailed off. Aubri heard footsteps and looked up to see Bastian and Aria approaching.

"Are you both okay?" Bastian asked. Nick turned to fully face him, nodding quickly.

"I'll be okay. I just...need time, you know?" Nick offered Bastian a weak smile, before a sigh left him.

"I get it." Bastian placed a hand on Nick's shoulder, squeezing it. "Take all the time you need. I'll be right here if you ever need to talk."

Aubri could only hope, as she watched Nick pull Bastian into a tight hug, that Nick wouldn't be too haunted by all that happened. That he wouldn't get nightmares of killing Reinhart like how she let Renee die. That he could move forward with peace.

She wasn't sure if she could, but she'd try.

CHAPTER 24

With the acting president dead and several other students and staff murdered in such a short span of a few days, the Da Capo Music Institution had no choice but to close for the rest of the semester after the news broke publicly. The staff could only hope that they found a new acting president if not someone to permanently take over the position. The official announcement, given by the school's board of directors, was that they hoped to reopen for the spring term with a new acting president.

Aubri doubted that anyone would apply to join the school too soon. She honestly wasn't sure how much longer the school would survive. At least, the public got some reassurance that Reinhart the killer was taken down. Aubri had a feeling that at least the school finally had a chance to put its murder-filled history behind it and look toward a better future.

Due to the school's closure for the rest of the term, Aria had no choice but to move out of her barely lived-in dorm room and head back home to her and Aubri's shared apartment for now. Bastian and Nick offered to help Aria pack up the supplies, which helped speed up the process. It only took less than an hour to grab all the things they needed and pack them into the couple of suitcases and bags Aria brought with her.

"I'm sorry that you barely got to start the term." Nick managed, looking towards Aria.

Aria shrugged, looking up at him. "At least we're still alive. All the tuition fees were moved to apply to next term, too, so it's not like I have to worry about paying again."

"I think it made sense for them to do so." Bastian quipped. "Forcing the students to pay again for another term when it barely started wouldn't be right."

"Besides," Aria offered them a soft smile, "At least this means I can stick with all of you for a while. And I already exchanged contacts with Akeno and Fen, so I can get to know some fellow classmates and other staff before we have classes."

Aubri smiled lightly at that. As Aria and Nick started talking to each other quietly, she looked towards Bastian. "How's Lulu – er, Louise, doing, anyway? Is she better?"

"I got a text from her earlier." Bastian admitted, shrugging. "She said she's getting released from the hospital by the end of the week, and should be fine. Got a lasting scar on her abdomen, though."

"I'm glad she's okay." Aubri heaved a relieved breath,

closing her eyes briefly. She thought of Nessandra, of how she quit her job at the resort after the near-massacre incident with Renee, and wondered if Lulu might continue working at this school despite the tragedies and near-deaths that occurred. A soft sigh left her afterwards as her eyes opened again. "I just… can't believe we've gone through all that, you know?"

"In a whole year and half, yes." Bastian couldn't stop himself from chuckling. "Do you think we've experienced enough?"

Aubri raised a brow. "Enough cases, you mean?"

"Yeah." Bastian looked her in the eye. "Look, I know we've gone through so much but – part of me wants to keep going. Keep solving cases and all that."

"Despite us nearly dying at least two out of three times?" Aubri couldn't stop herself from smiling, despite asking that.

"Yes. Is that so weird? I mean," Bastian ran a hand through his hair, "I guess it's just that we've been doing it for so long now that it's almost commonplace for us to encounter murders."

"Just like any other murder mystery novel we've read? Every show we've watched?"

"Just like a show, yeah." A soft laugh left him at that. 'I doubt we'd be consulted for any cases, but…whatever happens, we have each other to talk to. To work through things. And I'm just glad we've got that."

Aubri felt a weight leave her shoulders – and she nodded, offering him a soft smile. "Yeah. We've got each other."

Whether they encountered any more chaos in the future, whether it be murders or otherwise, at least she had Aria. She had Bastian and Nick. There were people in her life that she could spend her time with – and confide in, no matter how tough things got. If she had them, she knew that losing hope in the future – whether it be a new case or something else – wasn't going to happen.

AFTERWORD

Thank you for reading "Bloody Fantasia," the last book in the *Harlow Mystery* series! It's been amazing to write the entire series and all Aubri and her friends' investigations and adventures, and just as equally amazing to share them with all of you readers.

If you'd like to keep up with my future works, please consider following me either through the links featured in this Carrd or listed below:

Website: https://clarislam.ca

Newsletter: https://buttondown.email/clarislamauthor

Bluesky: https://bsky.app/profile/clarislamauthor.bsky.social

Facebook: https://www.facebook.com/ClarisLamAuthor

Instagram: https://www.instagram.com/clarislamauthor

Tumblr: https://clarislam.tumblr.com/

Bookbub: https://www.bookbub.com/profile/claris-lam

Goodreads: https://www.goodreads.com/author/show/22277014.Claris_Lam

ABOUT THE AUTHOR

Claris Lam

 Claris Lam (she/her) is an author and poet. Her first book, "Winner Takes All," was released on June 14th, 2022, and the sequel, "Engagement To Die For," was released on June 20th, 2023. "Bloody Fantasia" is the third and final book in the Harlow Mystery series.

She is currently writing several other novels, short stories, and poems. Her works have been published by literary magazines and organizations including INKspire and We Have Food At Home. You can learn more about her work at https://clarislam.ca

BOOKS IN THIS SERIES

Harlow Mystery series

Winner Takes All: A Harlow Mystery

Aubri Harlow thinks she's found her dream vacation after winning a contest to an exclusive island resort for a whole week. However, her dream quickly turns into a nightmare when her ex-boyfriend Colin, ex-girlfriend Renee, and former university classmate Bastian end up on the same island as fellow contest winners.

Even worse? Colin is found dead barely a day into the vacation. Terrible weather prevents the police from arriving on the island to investigate. To keep herself safe, as well as her other companions, Aubri must find out who the killer is...or risk becoming the next target.

Engagement To Die For: A Harlow Mystery

"Engagement To Die For" brings family reunions, dark secrets and histories revealed, and more murder where "Winner Takes All" left off!

After everything Aubri went through at the resort, the last thing Aubri needs is more drama. However, meeting her previously-unknown twin sister for the first time, and attending her mother's engagement party, results in yet another murder.

Due to the remote area of this crime, the police won't be able to make it for a few days. Aubri realizes that she, along with her friends and her sister, must take up the mantle themselves to solve the case or risk being new victims again.